PRAISE FOR *AFRICAN TOWN*

**A 2022 NPR BOOKS WE LOVE
SUMMER READING RECOMMENDATION**

**A 2022 GREAT READS FROM GREAT PLACES
READING LIST PICK (ALABAMA)**

"*African Town* is a stunningly powerful and visceral novel."

—Oprah Daily

"A haunting, beautifully told history."

—NPR

★ "Inspired by the true story of the last American slave ship, *African Town* is an epic . . . compelling novel that doubles as an important historic document, invaluable for both classroom use and independent reading."

—Booklist, starred review

"An ambitious verse novel told in many voices . . . The authors employ a range of poetic forms, resulting in an insightful, quickly paced telling that centers tradition and resilience."

—Publishers Weekly

★ "The authors have done a remarkable job of weaving the stories of the characters together and telling the story from both the perspective of the slaves and the people who orchestrated their purchase. Though this story is fictional it is based on a vast amount of research that was done on the actual people who participated in this story . . . This story will inspire readers to do some research to find out more about the real events that took place . . . Not to be missed."

—School Library Connection, starred review

"A thoughtful portrait of how trauma informs and inhibits identity making. The end matter is a wealth of fascinating information, from the author's note that details Waters and Latham's research process, to a list that elaborates on the characters' lives, to an account of what modern day Africatown (formerly Africa Town) looks like."
—*The Bulletin of the Center for Children's Books*

★ "*African Town* is a book that should be both taught and treasured."
—*BookPage*, **starred review**

"The highly personal stories in verse reveal the different aspects of this illegal trade and the impact on both the Black enslaved people and the White crew members . . . The Africans' attempts to hold true to their home cultures and traditions—most were Yoruba—as they try to adapt to their new reality come across most powerfully. Enhanced by rich back matter, this is a strong addition to literature about slavery."
—*Kirkus Reviews*

★ "This gripping novel . . . [is] told from the perspectives of a myriad characters directly and indirectly involved in this event . . . where each unique voice contributes to the greater whole. Carefully executed passages appear in various forms of free verse and poetry, and each one is specific to the particular character represented. This choice makes the individual contributors not only come alive but also stand out from one another as the narrative progresses. Extensively researched and purposefully designed, this book brings together details of events from 1859 to 1901 and culminates in several pages of back matter that reinforce the entire work. VERDICT This honest, heartrending, and inspiring story is an important and necessary contribution to historical fiction collections for young adult readers."
—*School Library Journal*, **starred review**

AFRICAN TOWN

AFRICAN TOWN

INSPIRED BY THE
TRUE STORY OF THE LAST
AMERICAN SLAVE SHIP

IRENE LATHAM & CHARLES WATERS

INTRODUCTION BY JOYCELYN M. DAVIS,
DESCENDANT OF *CLOTILDA* SURVIVORS

putnam

G. P. PUTNAM'S SONS

G. P. PUTNAM'S SONS
An imprint of Penguin Random House LLC, New York

First published in the United States of America by G. P. Putnam's Sons,
an imprint of Penguin Random House LLC, 2022
First paperback edition published 2023

Visit us online at penguinrandomhouse.com.

THE LIBRARY OF CONGRESS HAS CATALOGED THE HARDCOVER EDITION AS FOLLOWS:
Names: Latham, Irene, author. | Waters, Charles, 1973– author.
Title: African Town / Irene Latham & Charles Waters.
Description: New York: G. P. Putnam's Sons, [2022] | Summary: Chronicles the story
of the last Africans brought illegally to the United States on the *Clotilda* in 1860.
Identifiers: LCCN 2021041737 (print) | LCCN 2021041738 (ebook)
ISBN 9780593322888 (hardcover) | ISBN 9780593322895 (ebook)
Subjects: LCSH: Africatown (Ala.)—History—19th century—Fiction.
CYAC: Novels in verse. | Blacks—Africa—Fiction. | Africa—Fiction.
Clotilda (Ship)—Fiction. | Slave trade—Fiction. | LCGFT: Novels in verse.
Classification: LCC PZ7.5.L39 Af 2022 (print)
LCC PZ7.5.L39 (ebook) | DDC [Fic]—dc23
LC record available at https://lccn.loc.gov/2021041737
LC ebook record available at https://lccn.loc.gov/2021041738

Printed in the United States of America

ISBN 9780593322901

1st Printing

LSCH

Design by Rebecca Aidlin
Text set in Maxime Std

For my Alabama friends and neighbors, especially the residents—
past and present—of Africatown. Thank you
for sharing your stories.

—I. L.

For all my ancestors who fought for a better life—
especially my late grandparents George E. Waters, Sr.,
Victoria Nottingham Waters, and William H. Bantom.

And for my Poetic Forever Friend, Irene,
for believing in me.

—C. W.

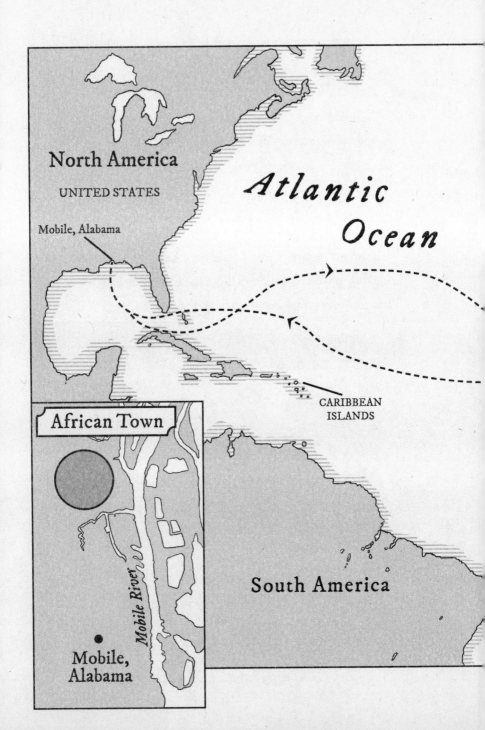

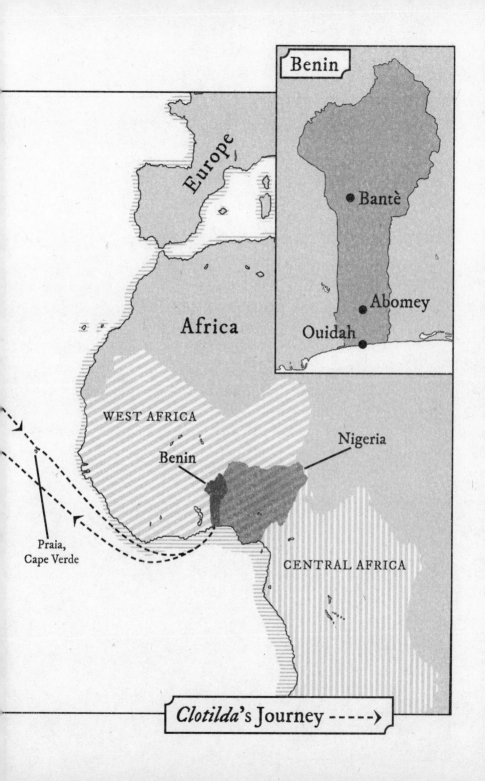

Benin

Bantè

Abomey

Ouidah

Europe

Africa

WEST AFRICA

Benin

Nigeria

Praia,
Cape Verde

CENTRAL AFRICA

Clotilda's Journey ----->

As for me, I will always have hope.

PSALM 71:14

CONTENTS

INTRODUCTION

When I was a teenager, my history teacher Mrs. Crocker asked, "Who knows their family history?" I raised my hand, and as my classmates looked at me, I lowered it. Would they make fun of me because my family was from Africa?

At the time, I wasn't ready to tell my story. But today I realize how important this story is—not just to me, but to the world.

My name is Joycelyn M. Davis. I am a direct descendant of Oluale, also known as Charlie Lewis, and Maggie Lewis.

I live and worship in Africatown. My family roots started in Lewis Quarters, where, collectively, a few of the *Clotilda* survivors saved their money and bought land from their enslaver. They established Lewis Quarters in 1870, and some of my family members still live there today. I work closely with other families whose ancestors also survived the *Clotilda*. I am the co-founder and vice president of the Clotilda Descendants Association and organizer of the Spirit of Our Ancestors Festival—a day set aside to honor our ancestors who survived the Middle Passage. It is my dream that this festival will grow and that people around the world will know about these courageous individuals I am proud to call my ancestors.

With that in mind, I encourage everyone to sit at your elders' feet and get as much information as possible. Take pictures, start a family tree, and make videos. Embrace your history, no matter how difficult it is. We are—*you* are—guardians of family history. We owe it to our ancestors to honor them as much as possible.

Now, when asked about my family history, I tell their story with pride! May their story inspire and enlighten you.

Thank you,

Joycelyn M. Davis
June 2021

AFRICAN TOWN

I.

HOME IS WHERE THE STORY IS

AFRICAN TOWN, ALABAMA, 1901

KOSSOLA

OUR STORY

Be still, my children. Listen with your ears
and your heart. Our story starts with this
mark on my right cheek, these chipped teeth.
See? This is how you know I am who I say I am.
De town where I was born is called Bantè.
It's nowhere near here, not in African Town, not
in Alabama. This town's way across de ocean,
on de west coast of Africa in de kingdom
of Dahomey. My family's home was a round,
two-story adobe with a terrace. Surrounded by hills,
about eight days' walk to de sea. Someday maybe
you will see de world de way I have seen it
in Bantè. Then you will know how de sun
kisses de earth, melts like honey over de land—
it's no wonder I believed all of life would be
bright and sweet. No wonder it still shocks me
that de world can be so hard, so dark.
But that darkness, it brought me here.
It brought *you* here. This is our story.

II.

DREAMS AND SCHEMES

WEST AFRICA AND THE UNITED STATES OF AMERICA, 1859–1860

KOSSOLA

MARKET DAY

My favorite day of de week is market day.
De market sits right in front of de king's
compound, which is located near de center
of Bantè. Villagers come from miles around,
passing through de eight gates in de tall
solid walls that enclose our town on all sides,
like a fortress. Dey come to buy goats, cows, yams,
fried wàrà, fùfú, palm roots, and yards of lace.
"Hurry up, ọmọ mi," my ìyá sings in Yorùbá,
like I'm still a child. She says I'll always be her
precious boy, even though I'm eighteen years
old now. "Your bàbá and bàbá àgbà
said you must rope the goats." I come from
a family of farmers—not royalty, but rich enough
to own our own animal herds. On market day,
all of us older children help out while
de younger ones race between de stalls
and bang homemade drums. When there's a lull,
I sneak away to find Adérónkẹ́, who waits for me
at de trunk of a mahogany tree. "Watch where
I put my feet," she says, scrambling higher
before my eyes can find her first foothold.
Her laughter rains down on me, soft
and shimmery. Teasing me, challenging me.
I grunt with my efforts, and when I slip,
I try again and again until I make it.
Together we watch de market from above,
two bright birds singing our own song

until de sun drops behind Bantè's walls
and de other villagers head for home.
"A good day," Bàbá àgbà says. We carry
only three cases of palm oil and two goats
back home. When I grab hold of de goats'
head-ropes, Bàbá àgbà puts a hand
on my brother Tayo's shoulder. "Stay close,"
he says, "or I will sell you to the Portuguese
for tobacco." Bàbá àgbà's eyes sparkle,
but his fingers hold firm. I throw my shoulders back,
keep my voice light. "Why would dey want Tayo,
when dey can have me?" We've all heard stories
about people getting snatched by King Glèlè's
soldiers and being sold to traders who carry them
across de sea. But that doesn't happen
in Bantè, with our walls and gates and families
all looking out for one another. Besides,
Bàbá àgbà doesn't even like tobacco.
Bàbá àgbà's cheeks lift, and he gives me
a playful shove. "Those traders don't want you,
Kossola. You talk too much." De goats follow
as Tayo and I pull ahead of Bàbá àgbà,
but not too far ahead.

TIMOTHY
MASTER OF DISGUISE

As the sun drops, I turn over the wheel of the *Roger B. Taney*
to my first mate so I can dress for dinner. Soon I'll join
my guests for drinks, smoking, and chatting. Oh, how
I love being on the water! Gives a man
a chance to dream, and to count successes.
And there have been many since I've moved to this state some
twenty-four years ago. Since then, me and my brothers Jim and Burns
dominate the shipping routes in Alabama. Our ancestors would
be dancing with pride.

As I gallop toward fifty years old, I've given my family's
name dignity—for my sweet, young wife, Mary, who isn't
but half my age, for our future children, and for my brothers, too.
As I enter the dining room, my guests greet me with respect.
"Good evening, Captain Meaher," they say.
"Evenin', everyone," I reply, tipping my hat.
I may be Irish by nationality, and a Mainer by birth,
but when necessary, I can transform myself into
either a Southern swashbuckler or a Southern gentleman,
depending on what's needed.

KOSSOLA

DREAMING OF ORÒ

For four years I've been training
to be a soldier, getting ready for my
initiation into orò, de highest level
of our Yorùbá religion. "I'm ready now,"
I tell Bàbá. He shakes his head.
"Soldier first. You must earn orò."
He hands me de spear, shows me again
how to settle my weight into my thighs,
reminds me to use my sight. "Keep your
eyes open, and the spear will follow."
I drop into de proper stance, but my mind's
stuck on orò. I want to be part of de secret
society of men *right now*. I don't want to wait
for de elders to say I'm ready. I *am* ready.
No one's more respected than de orò.
Dey decide which punishment fits which crime.
De king may have ultimate say,
but even he listens to de orò. I want to know
what it's like to sit in de woods for days
with fellow orò, deciding de fate of others.
I want to know that kind of respect and power.
Even de market shuts down and waits
for de orò's return. "Higher," Bàbá instructs,
and I lift de spear. If I can't make de years pass
any faster, at least I've got this time alone
with Bàbá. Perhaps I can impress him,
convince him I'm ready. My eyes zero in
on de target, and I heave my spear.

TIMOTHY

THE BET

The smoky room turns from laughter to seriousness
faster than a water-wheel when our conversation spins
to Congress's refusal to reopen the international slave trade.
I pound my fist on the table. "How do they expect us
to make a living? We need slave labor, and we need it cheap."
The gentlemen nod their heads, and talk
swings to the possibility of our state, and others,
seceding from the Union. "We *should* secede," I argue.
"Handle our own slave trade, set our own prices.
It's the only way to turn a profit."

Mr. Deacon, a businessman from New York City,
shakes his head. "Well," he says, "until that happens,
the threat of being lynched will disabuse anyone of
notions about bringing slaves in illegally."
I cough his words away. "Deacon," I say.
"You put more faith in the government
than I do. No one's going to lynch *me*."

Mr. Ayers, another Northeasterner, who specializes
in the production of pills, pipes up. "You can't bring Africans
within sniffing distance of America without being caught."

Mr. Matthews, a Louisiana farmer of the highest order,
shouts, "Of course it can happen. Matter of fact,
I'll bet you all a hundred dollars!" Well, that gets my attention.
"Gentlemen," I say, my voice ominous as a windless sky.
"I'll wager you all a thousand dollars
that I can smuggle a good number of slaves back
to Mobile without the authorities knowing about it."

The room erupts with shouts and laughter,
before we all shake hands to seal the bet.
Hang me? Let the government try.
A bet is a bet—and I aim to win.

KOSSOLA

SCARS

When de elders take de blade to
my cheek, I keep my eyes wide open.
My breath comes in quick huffs, but
I don't cry out. It's an honor to be marked.
And when, by firelight, dey tell me to open
my mouth wide, I pretend to be a hippo
as dey chip away at my top and bottom
front teeth. It takes a while for them
to finish. When I press my teeth together,
it makes a circle-shaped opening just big enough
to poke two fingers through. De marks
guarantee my place in Bantè and among
all Yorùbá people. Dey tell de world
I'm a skilled soldier—able to track, hunt,
and protect. I can throw spears, shoot arrows,
and set up camp. I'm not trained
to be a fighter—only to defend, to survive.
When de scarification is complete, Bàbá
looks me straight in de eye, pride lighting
his face. His expression tells me I'm becoming
a true Yorùbá man. De marks prove I'm exactly
where I'm meant to be—on de path to orò.

TIMOTHY
MAN WITH A PLAN

In town even the grocery clerk has heard about the bet.
"Captain Meaher," he says. "Why are you doing this?
Seems like a bad idea." I press my lips together,
make myself smile. "Thank you for your concern, sir."
His words only offer further fuel for me to succeed
at this challenge. Besides, slavery is as righteous
as Sunday morning.

I'm primed to right this wrong in my own way.
My business won't allow me time away to make this journey,
so first, I must reel in a captain—and the fish I want
to land is one William Foster. He and I
have been through some trials at sea together
that would have broken even the toughest of men. I respect him.
Also, he's a decade younger than me, which makes him
easier to manipulate, if need be. Doesn't hurt that
he's an immigrant, like my father. He aims to rise in
social status, which makes him eager to please, and even
more eager to make money. Besides, it'll give the poor man
a break from the Alabama pollen.

"Join me for breakfast," I say with a grin. Doesn't take
longer than two seconds for Foster to take the bait.

WILLIAM
BREAKFAST TALK

Captain Tim has hardly taken a breath
since we sat down. That man plows through
life like a ship's hull through water. My eyes
about pop when he makes his offer.
It intrigues me. For all his bluster,

Captain Tim doesn't let anything
get in the way of his goals.
I respect that. Always have.
It would be nice to get back at sea.
See if we can pull this off.

"I trust you, Foster," he says. "You may hold
Canada in your blood, but your heart's more
American than the Constitution." My chest
rises. I stick out my hand. "Captain,
it would be my honor to serve!"

Captain Tim's grin is as warm as his handshake.
"All we need now," he says, "is a ship."
I nod, and we both say in unison, "The *Clotilda*."
He claps me on the back. "Great minds think alike."
I'm about to bust with pride. "Here's to the *Clotilda*!"

CLOTILDA
CALL ME *CLOTILDA*

I'm docked opposite Mobile in a shipyard at the foot of St. Anthony Street.
I rock against my ropes as Foster and his men give me my riggings.

Just shy of my fifth birthday, I'm 86 feet of oak and pine planks, fastened
by iron. I carry with me the history of all vessels, the memory of all seas.

I've known a thousand different skies, every kind of storm and squall.
I know the weight of silence. And I know exactly what Foster and Meaher

intend when they tell everyone I'm a schooner to be used for lumber trade,
that I will prove graceful and fast. Yes, I am graceful and fast. But all else? Lies!

Meaher pays Foster $35,000 for my services, then loads my ground tier
with 125 barrels of water, 4 tubs of bread, 25 casks of rice, 30 casks of beef,

40 pounds of pork, 3 barrels of sugar, 25 barrels of flour, 4 barrels of molasses.
Enough for a full crew and a shipload of Africans for eight weeks.

Like it or not, I'm part of the illegal slave trade, a vessel of complicity.
I sit in horror of what's to come. For Foster and Meaher, it's full steam ahead.

TIMOTHY

A POINT OF CONTACT

As work progresses on the *Clotilda*, Foster and I
meet regularly to discuss our venture. "From which port
should we collect this cargo?" Foster asks as we tuck
into fried catfish with turnips and mustard greens.

I take a swig of malt liquor. Much as I'd like
to go big in Angola and Congo,
that's too far south for a ship the size of *Clotilda*.
We can't blow our cover. "We need a smaller port,"
I say to Foster.

"What about Ouidah?" he says. "In Dahomey?"
I tap my finger on the table as I recall an article in the
Mobile Register describing Ouidah as one of the best ports
along West Africa's Slave Coast.
"Yes," I say. "Ouidah it is."

KOSSOLA

DE SECRET OF DE GATES

It's Ìyá whose eyes fill with tenderness
when I lift little Tayo onto my shoulders
to make myself appear bigger, stronger.
"You have always reached for more,"
she says. "You wanted to live when all
those others didn't." That's why she
named me Kossola, which means "I do
not lose my fruits anymore." As Bàbá's
second wife, Ìyá needed me—a child—
to prove her worth to de family. Now
our house is full of many children.
"Size isn't what matters," Bàbá àgbà says.
He taps my head with his forefinger,
then rests his palm on my chest. "This is
what matters." My heart. I carry his words
with me as I hike alone to my post at one
of de eight town gates. It's part of my training
to guard de gates along with my older brother
and de other young men. As de hours pass,
I drag my bare feet in de dirt, wishing
I could climb de mahogany tree with Adérónkẹ́.
This is my job now, and it's important, yes.
But mostly it's hours I can fill with daydreaming.
Because no one messes with Bantè.
But one night as I stand guard, I detect
a rustling when there is no wind. De ground
vibrates just enough to tickle my toes,
sending my heartbeat skittering like a beetle

into my ears. I don't waste a moment—
I whistle de alarm. Families pour out
of their houses, heading for safety in de woods.
By evacuating, we might foil our invaders,
leaving them to find only an empty town.
My heart crashes as I wait with my family.
What if I'm wrong? What if I'm right?

TIMOTHY

INVESTMENT

Watching the *Clotilda*'s transformation, I almost wish
I was the one going over to capture those slaves.
But the ocean isn't for me. I'm a river man.

I know some of these old-money Mobile businessmen
have their doubts about my plan. I can't wait
to prove them wrong. It's not just a bet.
It's important for a man to invest in himself,
to diversify his ambitions. How else will he get ahead?
It's important that I leave a legacy for my family.

Next order of business is to find some sailors
who will sign up for this slave-trading job.
I'll have Foster deal with that.

J. B.

MARINER

Been an orphan since I was ten.
My parents cut and run when I kept
getting in trouble with the law in Rhode Island.

Became a stowaway on a ship called
Triumphant. When I was found out, they
put me to work in the kitchen.

Been hopping from ship to ship ever since.
Now, fifteen years later, I've worked my way
up to second mate. After two days on shore

at the Port of Mobile I ask about work.
"Captain Foster needs men," a seaman
says. "He's taking out the *Clotilda.*"

I jump at the chance. I've been ashore
too long. I need to feel the swells beneath
my feet—and fill my empty pockets.

It's a regular shipping job, which is fine
by me. There are only two things
about ship work I can't tolerate.

One: People who tell a thumper.
Two: Being anywhere near a slave ship.
Trouble brews on those dark vessels.

KOSSOLA

GOOD NEWS

Thanks to my quick action,
de attack is thwarted before
de intruders even reach our gates.
Our soldiers send them running
in de other direction. Before daylight
we are all safely back in our homes.
"Kossola," Bàbá àgbà says. "Thanks
to your good instincts, no one in Bantè
was hurt. The final phase of your initiation
to orò will now begin." I leap into de air
like a waterbuck crossing a stream.
"Mo dúpẹ́, mo dúpẹ́, mo dúpẹ́,"
I say. Thank you, thank you, thank you.
Across de room where she sits
with her stitching, Ìyá smiles,
showing all of her teeth. She's proud, too.
I can't believe it. Finally, it's official.
After years of training, now I am
one step closer to orò. Bàbá waits
for me to settle before telling me de rest.
"Tonight you'll stay at the initiation house."
Finally my future unfolds.

TIMOTHY

THINKING AHEAD

While Foster's out making last-minute preparations,
I go about my business, same as always. Evenings and Sundays
I share with Mary and my brothers. But even as I eat, drink,
smoke, and sleep, my mind whirls, searching for answers.
How in the world will I get away with it?
How will I hide these jigaboos once they arrive on Grand Bay?

And then, one crystalline dawn on the river, it comes to me:
I'll hire Hollingsworth, tugboat skipper extraordinaire,
to bring in my shipload once it reaches shore.

I'll line it up same as Foster's done the crew:
by promising healthy payment—and not revealing
what commodities lie wedged inside until it's too late.

Either way, after getting those Africans off my ship,
I'll hide them in the swamplands before
picking my favorites and selling the rest off.

Once all that is done, I'll clean up, retrofit, rename,
and reuse the *Clotilda*. A businessman knows not
to let a valuable thing go to waste.

KOSSOLA

LEARNING

Nothing makes me happier
than nights at de initiation house.
Each time I learn something new.
On this night, a strange roaring noise
comes from beyond Bantè's walls.
Not an animal, I don't think. But I'm
not sure. "It is up to you to find
the source of the sound," one of de elders
says. I look everywhere, but de noise
keeps moving and changing—
first, close and sharp. Next, far-off
and thunder-deep. I stomp my feet
in frustration. Why can't I figure it out?
When I get back to de initiation house,
de joke is on me. "This is a rhombus,"
one of de elders says. It's a big stick
with strings attached. "We use it
as a tool to foil our enemies. And to
communicate our strategies to one
another without using words."
De elders show me ways to make
different sounds by moving de sticks.
It's a language all its own.
Sharp, rapid shakes mean "Danger!"
and soft rustles signal "We're safe."
I impress de elders with my determination.
"Keep up the good work," dey say,
"and soon it will be time for your first
initiation ceremony."

CLOTILDA
DEPARTURE

Nighttime is quiet, except for the crickets singing their evening lullabies
as I bob in the Chickasaw Bogue. My masts stretch to the stars now,

my body's wider than the HMS *Indefatigable*. My bottom level has been
refashioned—better keep your body bent belowdecks or you'll smash your head.

Foster sneaks in like a thief with a bag slung across his back. As he stashes
it behind a loose flap of retaining wall, I smell gold. I know what he's up to.

Sure as I'm resting gentle on the water, he's going to use that gold and probably
a few other resources to bribe officials and to purchase human cargo.

In less than an hour the eleven-man crew files in. Foster double-checks
the papers he must show the authorities at every port. Falsified words

state we're bound for Saint Thomas with a supply of lumber. By first light
the crew is at work, and we're slicing swells across the Gulf of Mexico.

WILLIAM

HISTORY

The Alabama shoreline disintegrates.
I pace the deck in nervousness.
After seventy-four hours at sea, I spy Cuba.
I marvel that a skinny Canadian like me
got put in charge of so righteous a scheme!

I ignore the odd ache in my bones.
Another sailor might call it a premonition. If word gets
out about the kidnapping, I hope it's not for years.
By then I'll be sitting in a saloon. Drinking rye
and whiskey. Telling wide-eyed faces at my table

about how I outsmarted the port authorities.
Well, me and Captain Tim. Though he might
have financed the bet, I'm the one on the
water. It's me leading a potentially mutinous
crew across temperamental oceans. Me.

KOSSOLA

INITIATION CEREMONY

At de annual orò initiation ceremony,
we stay outside Bantè for nine days.
De first night, we gather around a fire,
and me and de other initiates
are offered a meal of roasted meat
and palm wine. I make myself eat,
even though my stomach's filled with bees.
No one's more excited than me
when de food's gone and de business
begins. "Do you vow to keep
the secrets of the orò?" dey ask.
"Yes," I say, and de elders present
me with a parrot feather—because
parrots are sacred in our Yorùbá culture.
Such a simple yet powerful symbol.
I spin de feather so it catches
de firelight, its soft shimmer
recognition for my hard work,
and a promise of good things to come.

J. B.

SEA LIFE

With Cuba behind us, it continues to be smooth
sailing. Captain Foster orders the crew to check
the running rigging and chafing gear,

braid rope-yarns, and do a host of other tasks.
From sunup to sundown it's one job after another—
just the way I like it. The only chance to think

is during a quick bite of boiled salt beef, rice,
and doughboys for dinner, then a few moments
on deck to enjoy my ration of ale.

Someday I'll set my own schedule, pilot my own ship.
I'm still trying to figure out Captain Foster.
For a man with so much experience on the ocean,

he's wound tighter than a typhoon. The sea
is a place to forget about your worries, to relax.
I guess we all have our problems.

If I could just stop wasting my money on liquor
and sporting women, I could save a little. Seamen
will clamor to set sail with me at the helm.

KOSSOLA

ADÉRÓNKẸ

I haven't yet completed my initiation
when my birthday comes—nineteen.
My mind, once so full of orò, expands
to include other things. When I watch
my parents working together in de garden,
their words so soft that only dey can hear,
I realize it's time for me to choose a wife.
And I know de one I want is Adérónkẹ.
I like de way she carries herself—back
straight, chin lifted, a smile in her eyes.
One market day, I'm so busy watching her
that I knock a bowl of wàrà into de dirt.
"Kossola!" Bàbá says. "Pay attention."
I wipe de wàrà so violently, de cake crumbles.
Later, I listen as my parents discuss my clumsiness.
"If Kossola doesn't wed soon," Bàbá says,
"we will lose all our customers." Ìyá glances
at me, then her eyelids drop. "So let it be done."
From my corner, I let out a whoop.
"As soon as you complete your initiation,"
Bàbá says, "you will be free to marry."
I bow and kiss them both. "De woman
I want is Adérónkẹ." Strong, proud,
tree-climbing Adérónkẹ.

WILLIAM
OFF COURSE

That's what I get for blowing sunshine
up my own trousers. One problem after
another hits in succession.
First, before we get to Bermuda,
I notice the *Clotilda* is sliding off her mark.

I try to correct her, but she won't stop
dancing. When we reach the dark
hours, I gaze at the stars for direction.
Yes, it's as I suspected. *Clotilda*,
you stubborn girl! Or—could it be

the reason for our navigational
problems might be the gold?
Could it be that the retaining wall behind
which I hid it when I boarded ship
is causing the compass to malfunction?

In the blue before sunrise, while my
men sleep, I sneak across deck.
When I remove the bag of gold,
the compass immediately rights
itself. Soon the *Clotilda* follows.

CLOTILDA

CONUNDRUM

If Foster hadn't figured out the hidden bag of gold near the compass
was causing me to slide away from our destination, I would have kept

sailing my way back to Mobile Bay. Foster and Meaher are both smart,
driven men—one an immigrant, the other a son of an immigrant—

both working themselves up from soil to stars. What good they could
do if they weren't so arrogant, so bent on profit and breaking the law.

I take comfort in the ocean that cradles me, the wind that sings to me,
and the sky that never abandons me—and I pray for forgiveness.

KOSSOLA

ọ̀YÉ

De season is marked by dry,
relentless northeasterly winds
that coat everything in dust. Doesn't
bother me—I like de silky touch
of it between my toes as I walk
through de town, alone, my initiation
into orò almost complete. Soon, I hope,
Adérónkẹ́ will walk beside me, and we'll
live with my parents, bring our own
palm oil to market, maybe even some
goats and a cow. A smile stays forever
on my face as I imagine de coming years
of sunshine and plenty. "I wish she
was already my wife," I say to Bàbá àgbà.
He scowls. "Don't wish your life away,
boy. Today is what matters." But me,
I'm always thinking about de future.
What surprises will it bring?

WILLIAM
DAYS OF FURY

March 17th. Our daytime skies are dark
as spilled ink. "Cyclone!" I shout.
Northrop hauls down the last sail
and we all take cover belowdecks.
For nine days we are tipped and tossed.

Clotilda sways and dips so violently
I can barely fashion a thought.
We lose all lifeboats save two.
The rudder head splits in three.
The fore sail splinters before the squall dies.

We then get ten hours of a
Portuguese man-of-war pursuing us.
We outrace it with an alacrity that causes
me shortness of breath to even recall.
Our ship is crippled. My crew is weary.

It's like we're human yo-yos.
There's no time to whine.
Must repair the *Clotilda*.
Keep the crew off my scent.
And above all: Stay the course.

J. B.
EYES WIDE OPEN

Well, what a holy mess this trip has been. A spot
of good weather, then hit by one storm after another,
not counting all these men-of-war. As if there's a target

on the *Clotilda* saying *"Please stop our ship."*
International patrols scout all vessels for possible
illegal activities, and it does nothing but delay our shipments.

Outgunning them may be fun for Foster, but it's misery
for the crew. He calls out directions while we work
ourselves to exhaustion. The air vibrates with strangeness.

When all settles, I still sense something is off-kilter.
Is Foster hiding something? I'm especially aware
of his eyes when I'm on the lower deck.

CLOTILDA
FORTY DAYS AND FORTY NIGHTS

Forty days and forty nights of Mother Nature's temper tantrums
in addition to a second Portuguese man-of-war have left me weary

and longing for a rest in some sun-drenched harbor. Foster, sensing
my lack of enthusiasm, makes a decision. "We'll stop in Praia,

give the old girl a rest." The crew lifts a cheer as high as the sails
and sets about their tasks with renewed fervor. As Northrop

heads belowdecks to patch my belly by removing slabs of wood,
he spies the excess of rum and pork. "What the devil?" he says.

Then his eyes grow wide, and I know he understands: There's no lumber
stored on this ship. Foster's outfitted me for transporting slaves.

If only I had words, I'd shout them out: *Revolt, crew, revolt!*
And to the Africans along the coast: *Run! They are coming for you!*

KÊHOUNCO

ON THE COAST

Before breakfast, my older sister Eniọlá smiles sweetly and links arms with me.

"Let's collect shells," she says, and we walk the shore, pocketing only the best ones. Today is Eniọlá's wedding day. "You're sixteen," she reminds me. "You'll be next."

"Things won't be the same," I say. She splashes me. "True. Soon they'll learn you are more than just 'the quiet one.'" I splash her back, and the waves cheer. "I get a husband," she teases, "and for a while you get our little sisters all to yourself."

J. B.

CONFRONTATION

That worthless piece of flesh lied! My face burns
with fury as I storm upstairs faster than a musket shot,
tell the men what kind of ship we're on.

We circle Foster on the deck. He clears his throat,
then offers a sober smile. "What's all this about?" As if
he doesn't know. I get in his face. "You put us on a slaver."

He lets out a stream of hot air filled with apologies.
"Unless you meet our demands," I say, "we're alerting
the Portuguese authorities." His face changes.

"What do you want?" Foster asks. Standing with
the crew makes me bold; I spew out the words,
"Double our pay." Foster doesn't miss a breath. "Done."

The air shifts as the crew nods their approval. Everyone
drifts back to work, appeased by the promise of money.
But something niggles my brain. Foster was too easy to sway.

KÊHOUNCO

BROKEN

I place my favorite shell with its pink spirals on the window ledge.

The rest of the day is a blur of wedding feast and dancing, and yes, me in charge of our three younger sisters, who can make mischief out of dust.

Our bed feels bigger without Eniọlá, which is good and not good. Moonlight finds the window, and I watch for it to catch the shell's spirals. But the shell isn't there— it's in three pieces on the floor. "It fell," my smallest sister says, and I pinch her, hard.

WILLIAM
QUID PRO QUO

Captain Tim is going to pitch an extreme fit.
Having to pay our crew double their
wages adds to the expenses.
Yet, faced with a guaranteed mutiny,
I know I did the right thing.

If I'd known how much energy all this deceit
would require, I'd have packed more brandy.
When we reach Portugal, the American
consul and Portuguese officials point
to the paperwork. "Where is your lumber?"

I'm forced to tell more lies. But their grim faces
soon rosy right up. I offer them Mobile's finest sparklers.
I give each dignitary's wife a fine scarf. It's enough
to persuade them to turn their gazes elsewhere.
We sail forth, ever closer to obtaining our human cargo.

KÊHOUNCO
PUNISHMENT

Mama says I must be the one to carry the water today—alone.

I'm still angry about the broken shell—nothing is safe with so many sisters.
And there's a hole in my day where Enịọlá used to be.

Instead of turning right for the well, I turn left toward the beach, retracing our steps
from the day before. This time I'll carry home a tiny shell. My sisters can't ruin what
they can't see. I will call it *Enịọlá*, and no one besides me needs to know about it.

III.

LIFE INTERRUPTED
WEST AFRICA, MARCH 1860

KOSSOLA

STORIES FROM ANOTHER COUNTRY

One morning Ìyá stays inside,
which isn't like her. "Are you feeling poorly?"
I ask. She presses her lips into a straight
line. "De air today tastes like it's from
another country." It's what she always says
when de dust sits thick and motionless.
"Probably travelers heading for de coast,"
I say. "De world is big." Ìyá shakes
her head. "This is the only world we need."
Her words roll through my mind as I check
de gates. Do all ìyás think de way
mine does, without imagination?
My life may be full of my family and orò
and Adérónké, but there's always room
for curiosity. To me de air tastes thick
with stories—stories I want to hear
and learn to tell—unless dey are about
King Glèlè. Those stories never have
a happy ending, except for Glèlè.

GLÈLÈ
RAID SEASON

Alone in
my throne room,
I am first

uncertain.
I may be
King Glèlè,

but I'm not
seasoned yet.
My father's

death feels fresh.
"Guide me," I
pray aloud.

Silence fills
the night, then
white lightning

splits the sky.
It hits me:
The spirits

are hungry.
Now that dry
season is

upon us,
and the time
draws near for

our yearly
festival
to honor

ancestors,
we must pack
the yards with

prisoners
to sell, to
sacrifice—

or else face
foul vengeance
of the dead.

"To the beach,"
I order
my soldiers.

"No captive
is too young."
And I wait.

KÊHOUNCO

ON THE BEACH

I face the ocean. "Show me the perfect small shell."

I reach for the shiny bit of white and blue and rinse it in the surf.
It sparkles like a night star in the bright, wet light.

I'm so busy admiring the shell and the waves are so raucous, I don't notice the men
approaching until they are close enough to grab me. I don't even have time to take
a step before the bigger man hoists me over his shoulder, like a sack of yams.

GLÈLÈ

FOR MY FATHER

Enough grief:
My waiting
days are done.

Tomorrow
night I'll lead
an attack

to honor
my father,
King Ghezo.

Two years now
since his death.
One fine way

to keep his
legacy
alive is

to capture
and sell more
prime slaves. For

what other
reason did
I choose my

name, "Glèlè,"
than to prove
I'm worthy

enough to
follow my
father? I,

too, can be
a strong king—
starting now.

KÊHOUNCO
PROMISE

When I scream, the man clamps his hand over my mouth.

"Be quiet, or we will kill your family." My heart clenches, and I stop screaming. The waves crash. "Please," I beg. "Just let me go home."

"We're taking you to King Glèlè in Ouidah," he says. "To sell." I kick then, thinking of Enịọlá, thinking of our sisters. But I don't dare mention them. I may be just cunning enough to get away from these men, but my sisters aren't.

GLÈLÈ

NIGHT MUSIC

My heart pounds
in time to
my men's feet

marching in
darkness to
Bantè. They

carry me,
because kings
should always

be lifted
to command
respect. Each

attack feels
the same, and
different:

I know we
will prevail,
but will they

be strong stock?
Will they fight
or concede?

My heart pounds
as we sneak
and surround.

Outside town
gates, my troops
kill two right

away—no
sound at all.
I whistle

long-short-long
and my men
take the gate.

They explode
into shouts,
their axes

swinging as
my father's
spirit fills

my soul with
a hunger
that can be

fed only
by certain
victory.

KOSSOLA

ATTACK STORY

I wake with a start, my hands reaching
for my spear. De hair on de back of my neck
lifts as I make out a sharp whistle and shouts.
"It's an attack!" I call, and our whole house
leaps into motion—Ìyá shepherds
de younger children into de back room,
and de rest of us run toward de gates.
My breath leaves me as soldiers pummel
de iron with their axes. Dey scream,
but all I'm able to do is stand there, frozen.
After all my training, my body is a dull blade.
I'm useless as de world around me
roils and boils. BOOM! De first gate falls.
Soldiers rush us, shoot their French guns—
POP POP POP! Dey butcher some people
with knives—SLICE! Nowhere to go,
nowhere to hide! Soldiers at each
of de eight gates, blocking us, taunting us.
And me, lifeless as my parrot feather
lost now in de night. I'm blindsided when
three tall soldiers seize me,
punch me, push me to de ground.
Their oiled skin glistens in de torchlight,
illuminating de markings I know to be those
of Glèlè's soldiers. Glèlè, king of Dahomey,
king of de slave trade along de Ivory Coast.
"Please," I beg. I don't know why Glèlè
would target Bantè when our king's

so generous with our crops. "Let me go
to my ìyá!" I know what dey will do to her,
to Adérónké̩. "Adérónké̩," I breathe, my eyes
searching for her. But de captors
have no patience. Dey rope my hands
and feet, tie me to another and another—
faces at once familiar and strange,
for none of them are from my family.
My chest heaves. Where are my parents?
Where are Bàbá àgbà and my siblings?
Where are dey? "Adérónké̩!" I cry.
"Ìyá!" My eyes flash wild as de soldiers
drag me along with de others.
De ropes burn my ankles. Still, I strain
to hear de voices of de ones I love.
"Bàbá, Ìyá, where are you?"
No answer, only screaming.

GLÈLÈ

WHEN KING MEETS KING

Bantè's king
strides toward
me, across

ground littered
with the dead.
He doesn't

waver. He
faces me.
"Why do you

come at night?
Can't those from
Dahomey

fight like men,
in daylight?"
My soldier

translates his
words into
my language.

I smile, shrug.
"I'm sending
you to the

barracoon.
You'll garner
a good price."

Bantè's king
plants his feet.
"You'll take me

nowhere. I'd
rather die
a king than

surrender."
We both know
one so bold

cannot live.
When I give
a sharp nod,

my soldier
swings his blade—
SLICE!—the king's

head thumps to
the ground just
before his

body slumps
into blood-
thirsty dirt.

KOSSOLA

MARCHING TO DE SEA

We march all night, each step carrying
me farther away from de tall walls of Bantè,
from de massacre, from my loved ones.
By de time de sun paints de sky peachy-purple,
I'm too weary even to cry. My ankles bleed,
but I will myself not to stumble. De way we're
tied to one another means we must all move
together, or else de whole line of us will fall.
More than once, we do fall, only to be poked
and prodded, yanked back up by de soldiers.
As de sky lightens, my eyes lift, find severed
heads hanging like ornaments from de soldiers'
belts. My stomach heaves. "Don't look,"
de man just ahead of me says. "Just breathe."
I notice he wears a small hoop earring in each
ear, and his upper teeth have been chipped
to form an inverted V—which means he's an
initiate of òrìsà, and just a few years older than me.
While de orò are busy guiding and protecting
de town, de servants of òrìsà devote themselves
to one of our gods. Dey also honor de spirits
of our ancestors. "You okay?" he asks, like he's
de big brother and I'm a little child. He tells me
his name is Kupollee. "Ku" means "death" in Yorùbá.
I swallow. "I just—I just want to see my family,
to know if dey are alive." Kupollee shakes
his head. "You must face this truth. If you haven't
seen them by now, they are surely dead."

My face crumples and my eyes turn wet.
I won't believe it. I can't believe it. De day
showers us in dust and heat, but no food or
water. My mouth turns gritty and my nose cakes.
Meanwhile, soldiers carry Glèlè on a covered
hammock, hand him mangoes, oranges,
papaya. When he's done feasting, he drops
de peelings onto de ground right in our path.
My stomach lurches as my feet shuffle
across that rainbow of rinds. I can tell by de way
de land flattens that we're heading southwest,
to de coast. I try to keep track, making a map
in my mind, so that later I can find my way home.
De soldiers bang their sticks against our backs
if we so much as grunt or turn a head. I focus
on where to put my feet, tell myself each step's
bringing me closer to something better. De best
thing I can do is stay alert, focused—
de way de orò taught me.

KUPOLLEE

FIRST NIGHT

At dark, the soldiers order us to
our knees, then onto our backs. My
heart hangs inside my chest like
a dry avocado
when I realize
they mean for us
to sleep on
dirt, like
goats!

How can they disrespect us this way?
I've always slept on a raised bed.
The one beside me whose name
is Kossola sniffles.
My cheeks burn with shame.
The earth smells of
loneliness,
decay,
death.

KOSSOLA

STRANGE COUNTRY

De next days and nights blur in my mind.
We're like ghosts, our minds scrambled
from degradation and lack of nourishment.
We stink from dirt and sweat and waste.
I'm glad when a man chained near me
speaks to both me and Kupollee. "My name's
Oluale," he says. "That's my bàbá's name,"
I tell him. Arrows of pain ping my chest
as I think of Bàbá. "I would hate for him
to see me like this," I say. Oluale nods
and shares about his own town, his own family.
But some of his words get swallowed by
de smell of rotting flesh rising from de severed
heads de soldiers carry. When de flies get thick
as thunderclouds, de army stops. Once we're
all on de ground for sleeping, dey build fires
and proceed to smoke de heads. De smoke
curls up, disappears into de night. For de first
time, I'm glad Ìyá's not with me. At least
she doesn't have to breathe de air of this country.
My eyes run out of tears. I just want to return
home, to Bantè. To go back in time. So that's
what I do. I turn my mind to Bantè, to market
days when I was just a boy banging a drum
and climbing trees with Adérónkẹ́. My whole
family there tending de crops and animals.
No soldiers or ropes or smoking heads.
My loved ones right beside me. Our faces
lit with joy.

KUPOLLEE

BARELY THERE

For nine days we stay in that same spot.
My heart still beats, but it's fragile
as a newly hatched chick's peep.
The soldiers march; we march.
"Next stop, Abomey!"
they shout at us.
Abomey:
Glèlè's
home.

KOSSOLA

PALACE OF SKULLS

De tall adobe walls of Glèlè's palace
are visible long before we reach them.
It seems impossible, but de building
itself stretches for miles. Our steps
quicken as we approach, and vibrations
rise from de earth and fill my body.
De noise of drumming and chanting
deafens me as we cross de wide ditch
surrounding de palace and ease through
an opening in de fortress of thorns.
We pass through de gate of an iron
fence adorned with skull after skull
after skull. De crowd erupts when dey
see us, and that's when I realize
we, de prisoners, are Glèlè's trophy.
I want to press my palms against
my ears, but de chains will not allow it.
I want to run, but that is an impossibility.
We don't stand a chance against
de supremacy of Dahomey. I can
barely see for de tears flooding my eyes
as dey march us past de throngs.
"Why are they doing this to us?" a woman
cries as dey force us into a stockade.
"If only our king had given Glèlè the corn
and yams, this wouldn't be happening."

But I don't think that's true. De skulls'
empty eyes tell me our king could've
given de entire crop of corn and yams.
That's not what Glèlè's hungry for.

GLÈLÈ

BLEMISH

My return
is sullied
only by

the sight of
my nephew
Gumpa. He

doesn't praise
me like all
the others.

His eyes grow
dark before
he turns his

back to me.
I won't have
him spoil this

moment with
his judgment
of my ways—

as if kings
can command
without force.

"Take care of
Gumpa," I
tell Akodé,

my loyal
nephew. On
this day I'm

not simply
a man. I
am a god!

GUMPA

SNATCHED

Uncle Glèlè never has liked me.

His eyes shrink in jealousy when people flock to me for advice
or crowd around to hear me speak of Dan Ayidohwèdo, the
rainbow snake symbol of the Fon.

He only wants followers, and I am as independent as a rhino.

I see he is just a man pretending to be a god.

Which is why I am not surprised when his most ruthless follower,
my cousin Akodé, springs out of the bushes when I am enjoying
the starlight on a moonless night.

Akodé leaps upon me, presses a knife to my throat, and clamps his
hand over my mouth.

I struggle, but I cannot get away.

My anger swells as he marches me to the barracoon.

It shames me to share the same blood as these people.

KOSSOLA

INSIDE DE STOCKADE

For three days and nights we sit
in de dark, our backs pressed against
one another, our stomachs grumbling.
Dey feed us gbÈgÌrÌ soup, and I slurp
it like a drunken goat. At least it's
something to take my mind off de wailing
and begging. "Please," de women call.
"Let us go home." De men cry out, too.
"Please," dey say. "We'll give you all
our crops." As if these soldiers want to hear
our promises. Dey beat us until we get
quiet. When dey hear so much as a sigh,
dey shove de smoked skulls in our faces.
I've got no more tears left for my family.
Dey are all drained out of me. I place
my hand on de shoulder of de one closest
to me—de òrìṣà man named Kupollee.
"Tell me about you," I say. Even though
we are both from Bantè, I do not know him.
"Do you have a wife?" He drops his eyes.
"Not anymore." My throat tightens.
It is too painful for him to talk about, so
he tells me about his garden, its long rows
kept clear of weeds with his own hands.
"The earth is what brings me peace. Dirt,
and growing green things." He speaks
of bringing things to life, to fruit. "I cannot
bring my wife back to life, but the earth

is always there." I'd rather listen to his words
than to those talking about their wishes for death.
Even locked in de terrible stockade, I do not
want death. I have always wanted to live.

GLÈLÈ
THE TASTE OF VICTORY

On the fourth
day after
my return,

the grand feast
begins. The
city comes

alive with
shouts, drumbeat,
and singing.

The raid could
not have been
sweeter! Yes,

my lips smack
just thinking
of the price

these captives
will fetch me
at Ouidah.

My father's
face appears
in the flames.

He smiles, and
I know he
is pleased by

my success.
But I can't
enjoy it,

not quite yet.
Time now to
appease the

keen spirits.
"I shall buy
these captives."

The ancient
ritual
requires such

pretense. See,
Father? I
respect you.

KOSSOLA

DE CEREMONY

De soldiers pull us forward in long lines—
at least Kupollee's right in front of me.
This time we're bound not with raggedy
rope, but smooth fabric-wrapped cord.
I stroke it as if it's a pet, until Kupollee shakes
his head. "A vine may be green as life,
but it can choke a tree." I cast my eyes down,
embarrassed. De softness of de rope isn't
for our comfort, it's part of de ceremony.
De crowd cheers as each soldier presents
Glèlè with a skull. In return, de soldier receives
a head of shells or a fathom of cloth.
I've never seen such bounty, even on
de richest market day in Bantè! And it doesn't
end there. For each of us living prisoners,
Glèlè offers de spirits even more extravagant gifts.
Kupollee spits. "Glèlè is all roar and mane,
just like his symbol the lion," he says.
He tells me that Glèlè believes he can claim
human lives as long as he gives
something valuable back. That de treasures
guarantee dey won't seek revenge.
As if de spirits are easily fooled, like me.

KUPOLLEE

TRIAGE

We
line up
after the
ceremony.
Officials inquire
about our lives, our health.
When I say, "Òrìṣà," their
eyes brighten like I am a prize
melon. "This one will bring us fortune."

KOSSOLA

NEW NAMES

We are shuttled through de sorting
process, moving from table to table.
When de man asks me, "What do you do?"
I say, "Farmer," because I can't claim
to be orò when I haven't completed my
initiation. De man says, "Then you will be
called 'Farmer.'" He writes it down in a book.
"But my name is Kossola," I say.
He glares at me. "Not anymore. Don't
need names in Ouidah." That's because
in Ouidah, men are sold and shipped
away from Africa. I stumble as he pushes me
toward de proper group. Just ahead of me,
at de table for de women, my eyes light
on a familiar set of shoulders and perfect
tree-climbing arms. My heart nearly takes flight.
"Adérónké?" She's here? She's *alive*?
"Adérónké," I shout. "Turn around! It's me,
Kossola." But when she faces me, it's not
Adérónké. Her cheeks are too full, eyes set
wide apart. No dimple in her chin. "My name's
Abilè," she says. My body folds in on itself.
It's not Adérónké at all. Still, I don't want
to leave her. I crane my head as de soldiers
push me forward, until Abilè's swallowed by
de crowd of bodies. I'm surrounded
by people, but I've never felt more alone.

ABILẸ̀
NOT JUST A PILE OF STONES

I stay with the group of women slated for Ouidah,
        where big ships wait to carry us away, forever.
I can't think about that, so I think about the one who calls
            himself Kossola. Part of me wishes

I was the woman he mistook me for—not a shameful
        fifteen-year-old girl who let herself get captured.
We're both being sent to Ouidah, so our paths are connected
           now. I don't comprehend the full meaning

until I see the pile of stones. It's a ritual for leaving.
        As we walk toward the pile, officials watch as each
of us grabs a stone from the path. Mine is smooth and fits just
            right in my palm. I rub it with my thumb—

long, hard strokes, until I am standing in front
        of the pile. "Goodbye," I whisper, goodbye to
my old life, goodbye to my home, goodbye to my family
           and friends, goodbye to *me*.

As the stone flies from my fingers and lands
        with a thud among all the others, I realize the pile
is not just for us. It's a monument, true. But the officials
           are also using the stones to count us.

I close the door on my sadness, my memories,
        my whole past life. Now I will be someone new.
I lift my chin, press my shoulders down.
           I will not look back.

GLÈLÈ

CENSUS

Each stone the
captives add
to the stack

represents
a number—
proof of the

power of
my kingdom,
Dahomey.

Do you see,
Father? This
tall tower

proves your might.
Each captive,
yours and mine.

Our kingdom
secure and,
yes, supreme.

KOSSOLA

MARCHING AWAY FROM ABOMEY

After I toss my stone onto de pile,
I follow de others and complete de ritual
by circling de pile three times. It shocks
me that Glèlè's officials allow it, but dey do.
"It makes their job easier," Kupollee says.
As much as I want to leave this place
with its ominous skulls, my feet drag.
"I just want to go home," I tell Kupollee
as dey march us away from de castle,
toward de coast. "It will take us days
to get to Ouidah," Kupollee says.
"It's at least fifty miles to Ouidah.
We'll likely go through Zogbodome,
Toffo, Allada." He points up. "See how
the sky sheds its pink for blue? Different
every time you look." He reminds me
it's de same in de garden. "Change is
the way of nature. How else would we
get fruit?" I know he's right, but my
longing heightens with each step.
"Don't you miss your family?" I ask.
"The earth is my family," he says.
"They can't take that away." His words
fill me with a welcome sense of peace
that lasts all along de route—even
through de stop at Zogbodome,
where we're examined by doctors.
Dey treat my rope burns with a salve

that sucks de heat right out. We rest
at Toffo, and again at Allada, just as
Kupollee predicted. When we reach Savi,
de soldiers gloat. "Last stop before Ouidah,
eight miles to the barracoon."
A low rumble of murmurs and sighs
passes through our group. Eyes widen
with fear and apprehension. We all
know about de ships in Ouidah—
de ships that take our people away.
But de barracoon is a separate nightmare,
a prison of horrors. All my cells tremble.
Kupollee again points to de sky. Its blue
is now blanketed by fat, billowy clouds.
Different again. My stomach settles
as I follow my friend
and press one foot in front of de other.

IV.

OUIDAH
MAY 1860

CLOTILDA
ARRIVAL

After ten weeks of fierce travel across these surges and swells, finally
we reach our destination. Foster docks me just off the coast of Ouidah.

As grateful as I am for the rest, as proud as I am of my performance,
I would give anything not to be here, not to be part of this terrible business.

Even the water smells of death, and I can only imagine how many more
lives will be lost aboard my decks and holds. If only there was a way

to prevent the inevitable—alas, I am just a ship, at the mercy of men
and wind and sea. I am no more free than the slaves soon to come aboard.

WILLIAM
THE WELCOME COMMITTEE

We arrive at 4:00 p.m. Set anchor
as waves slash and crash the hull.
A black man in an outrigger appears.
Time for me to get down to cases.
I must keep up this facade of kindness.

"May I help you, mister?" he says.
I conjure a smile. "Good day, fine sir.
I'm Captain William Foster of the *Clotilda*.
I'd be most grateful to meet your ruler
for a possible purchase of slaves?"

He turns, signals to the shore.
Soon a paddled boat, long as daylight,
arrives, and I—not kidding—get into
a hammock fastened to the heads of
two men. It comes complete with

an awning to block the sun from my face.
Now, that's what I call service! As we
cross the mile and a half to shore, I grin.
I can say, without a scintilla of doubt,
you don't get this kind of welcome in Mobile.

KUPOLLEE

STOCKADE

One
small house
holds us like
limes in a straw
basket. Market day
is coming, sure as waves
crash—free—outside. They feed us
rice, shackle us in iron neck
fetters. Chain us. How the ocean moans!

KOSSOLA

LISTENING TO DE OCEAN

Before de barracoon we are shoved
into small, fenced pens. At least I'm placed
next to Kupollee and another—a Fon
called Gumpa—whose deep rumbly voice
steadies me. "They will not kill us," he says.
"We are worth more alive." He tells us
how his own cousin was de one to
kidnap him. "That may be," Kupollee
says. "But they can't chain the whole
world. The ocean and the earth will always
be free." He instructs us to find de ocean
in our minds, to listen to its music—
not to de hollering inside de pens as new
groups of men and boys are brought in
from other towns. But I'm hungry
for news of Bantè, of my family. What if
my older brother's there, in de building
dey call a barracoon? Or Tayo. I call
their names, but neither answers.
Where's Abilè, and all de other women
who put their stones on de pile in Abomey?
Are dey shackled, too? I turn to Gumpa.
"How long can dey keep us like this,
in de mud and heat?" Gumpa's eyes soften.
"Imagine the night sky," he says. "Stars speak
the language of the free." After a while,
soldiers move us inside, to de barracoon.
At least there's a roof. Voices become

less desperate, friendlier. We even play
games in de barracoon. Grown men acting
like boys, jumping up to spy things outside
de high windows. It's true de ocean doesn't
stop being de ocean, and even locked up,
we don't stop being people.

GUMPA

BROTHERS-IN-ARMS

My mind goes back to when Cousin Akodé kidnapped me.

I know if he had not snuck up from behind with his knife against my throat, and instead fought me man-to-man with our fists only, the outcome would have been far different.

I tamp the memory down and try to focus my attention instead on this new attachment I feel for both Kossola and Kupollee.

These two young men—who could be my little brothers—have gentle dispositions that may make them vulnerable.

I call upon Dan Ayidohwèdo to protect us all.

Our spirits connect us regardless of these white men trying to beat down our greatness.

KÊHOUNCO
NEW ARRIVALS

I've been in the cage a week, my cunning starved and beaten out of me—

when instead of marching us out for our daily walk, the men march in
a long line of women and girls. My heart leaps, and I rush toward them.

"Mama? Eniọlá?" I want so badly to see my family—even my destructive
little sisters! I look at each face, but none of them is familiar. Not one.
All of them ignore me, except a girl around my age. "My name is Abilẹ̀," she says.

ABILẸ

BARRACOON

So many women! But I have eyes only for the one
      with the bright, hopeful eyes. She reminds me of—no,
I will not allow my thoughts to go backward.
           I make my voice extra gentle. "What is your name?"

She braces her legs. "Kêhounco," she says, and her lips tremble.
      "They caught me at the beach." She pulls from her
pocket a tiny, perfect shell. "It's beautiful," I say. She tucks
      it safely away, her eyes wet now.

We share our ages—she's got sixteen years to my fifteen.
      She tells me about Eniọlá's wedding, and how
her sisters angered her. I simply listen as she circles back
      to the beach. "I tried to get away—" She swallows.

"It's my fault. I was supposed to fetch water, not go to the shore."
      Her eyes fill with tears. I tilt her chin like an ìyá would,
make her meet my eyes like a bàbá would. "Kêhounco," I say.
      "It's not your fault. You were kidnapped."

I hug her like a sister would, and she melts into me for a brief
      moment before she pulls away, straightening like a corn stalk.
"Stay with me," she says, her voice hardly a whisper.
      "Please. We'll be safer together."

KÊHOUNCO
SMALL WORLD

For now—until I can escape—Abilè with her steady arms will be my Eniolá.

When the men shackle us to move us out of the barracoon, the women cringe and cry. A little girl, probably not more than two years old, won't stop sobbing.

I bury my head in Abilè's neck, glad my sisters are not in this awful place. "I'm here," she says, and a hum creeps out of her, blocking the noise, the pain. I clasp my shell— the only thing I have left of home. My life shrinks to the circle of me and Abilè.

WILLIAM
AKODÉ

After sleeping on a bed soft as angels' wings,
I'm picked up by an interpreter.
We hike to another dwelling to meet
Chodaton Akodé. He's the one in
charge of negotiating a price for the slaves.

"Akodé is the nephew of Glèlè, king of
Dahomey," the interpreter informs me.
Sweat dampens my armpits as we wait.
When Akodé arrives, everyone prostrates.
He's a husky, towering man with skin darker

than anthracite. We imbibe fermented potions
to much laughter before getting down to brass
tacks. "I offer you $100 apiece for 125 Africans.
I'm prepared to pay in commodities and gold," I say.
Akodé rubs his chin. Considers my offer.

"You must give me time to discuss it with
the king," he says. "Please allow my men to
give you a tour of our precious land." My face
breaks into a smile. "Yes," I say, anticipating how
tales of this adventure will impress Captain Tim.

KUPOLLEE

RESCUE EFFORTS

Strange
voices,
languages
even I don't
know. One prisoner
is freed when his father
offers the guards a bag of
oranges and a fat milk cow.
Another is exchanged. But not us.

WILLIAM
WAITING

My hay fever has let up. So, I take
long walks. Admire the foliage and listen to
insects chattering. Drink myself groggy.
I ingest more movable feasts than
my skinny frame can allow. One afternoon

my interpreter takes me to a holy place.
A stone wall writhes with serpents.
As part of their ritual, he demonstrates how
the snakes are used to encompass each person's
abdomen and scruff. It's the strangest thing.

I'm ready for Chodaton Akodé to get back to
me. It's been eight long days. I hardly have
any fingernails left from all my chewing.
Paranoia bites at my bones.
Have I become a prisoner?

KOSSOLA

HOPE

When I see de families
coming to free their loved ones,
I know Bàbá àgbà would give
de cows and crops and everything
to get me back. "I know dey
will come for me," I tell Kupollee.
If dey can. If dey are alive.
"They aren't coming," Kupollee says.
"Not every yam seed grows
into a plant that will produce yams."
He's not trying to be cruel,
just practical. "You know de language
of yams, too?" I tease him. He knows
many languages. But Kupollee,
who's older by a few years,
wiser, and òrìṣà—there's no way
he can know everything. I'm not
ready yet to give up. "Rest," he says.
"Even dirt must rest between crops."
His earrings glitter as dey catch
de light. And you know, despite chains
and fetters, I *do* rest. Because
Kupollee lets me lean against him—
a bit of softness in a hard, dark place.

WILLIAM

TO THE BARRACOON

Day nine of waiting. There's a thump
at my door. It's the interpreter with news
of Chodaton Akodé wishing to see me.
"Bring payment," he instructs. When I get there,
the prince sticks out his hand. I offer him money

with the promise of our shipload of barrels
full of gold and commodities. He takes the initial
payment with a smile and a nod. No words.
It happens so quickly I wonder if he's an
apparition. Two men, in addition to the interpreter,

escort me to the barracoon, where my cargo awaits.
I press my handkerchief to my nose. The odor
blooms as we walk inside. So many coal-black
bodies! Most are naked. Others wear clothes so
ragged I wouldn't even use them to scrub

the *Clotilda*. One of my escorts speaks.
"You've bought the right to select 125
captives." If only I didn't have to inspect them!
It's the same tedious procedure as when buying
a horse. I take a deep breath and get to work.

KOSSOLA

WHITE MEN

De first time I see men with white skin,
I think dey must be spirits. Dey don't
look real to me with their stringy hair
and color variations of pale, ruddy,
and blotchy. But I soon find out how
real dey are by de way dey poke and prod,
not a bit of kindness in their faces—more
like de way Bàbá àgbà's forehead would
crease and his jaw would set when he was
weeding de garden—all business.
No time for fooling around. At first I'm too
busy being curious to be scared. Then
an image of de orò in de woods flashes
across my mind. Dey would tell me
to pay attention, because fear is sometimes
de very thing that keeps us alive.

KÊHOUNCO

WHITE SURPRISE

I stay close to Abilè, our skin always touching.

When the white men come in, she gasps and clenches her eyelids closed. As they rip clothing from others, I shift my shell from my pocket to my mouth.

It's true their white faces are shocking as a cold bath, yet part of me wants to see them, so I crack my eyes into slits. I want to know what I'm up against. I just don't want them to notice me, or Abilè.

ABILẸ
MYTHS AND LEGENDS

We have words for white men: *yovu, anasara,*
       bature, ọkùnrin òyìnbó. All my life I've been told
white people eat people. I shudder, but make myself
          stand tall and strong, for Kêhounco.

"Shhhh," she soothes, her palm sister-like against my cheek.
       Our captors' pale skin makes me want to turn
away, but I hold steady. I promise myself that
          this new me in this new life

will shrink for no one or nothing. Kêhounco has lost
       just as much as I have, and still, she stalks quiet, yes,
but determined as a cheetah. I grip her hand, and she doesn't pull away.
          Maybe the white men will eventually eat me,

maybe they will make gunpowder of my bones.
       But I will not make it easy for them. "Look at his long nose,"
Kêhounco whispers. "Like an anteater." For a moment
          the weight of my fear dissolves into giggles.

KOSSOLA

CIRCLES OF SHAME

De white men use an interpreter to tell
us to make circles of ten men each.
Dey go circle to circle, placing themselves
right in de middle. De skinny little man's
de one in charge. I can tell by de way
he points and pokes. By de time dey get
to our circle, I know his name's Captain Foster,
or Foster, for short. I look at my feet
as he examines de others in my circle.
I can't watch him put his hands on their
arms and legs, his fingers in their mouths
and private places. Foster does de same
to me. It's so shameful I wish a hole
would open and swallow me into de earth.
Afterward, he points at me, and de other
white men pull me from de circle. Kupollee's
pulled, too, and comes right behind me.
After three weeks of waiting in Ouidah for
something to happen, my stomach clenches.
I don't know what we've been chosen for,
but at least being chosen means our story
doesn't end here; we're moving on
to de next chapter.

ABILẸ
SISTERS BY CHOICE

My heart shakes like a coconut tree
        during harvest, but I don't allow Kêhounco
or the white men to see. I stand tall, firm. I force
          myself to look at the one they call Foster

right in the eye. He punishes me for it
        by squeezing my breasts. But I don't
grimace. I pretend to be a stone and pray
        my small act of defiance

helps them pass over Kêhounco quickly.
        I am not surprised when Foster points,
selecting us both. Kêhounco lifts her chin,
        nods at me like we have won something,

who knows what. "Come, sister," she says, as if we are
        the ones making this decision. "Yes, sister," I say.
We may be only two, but dignity is easier to muster as a team.
        My heart settles when she grips my hand.

WILLIAM
SELECTIONS

Being thorough in picking out
my cargo doesn't necessarily mean
going slow. I know what I want.
This makes the process go faster than
seagulls diving for crabs. I check any and

all of the Africans' orifices, disgusting
as it is. I'm grateful they're already
shaved. There'll be no venereal
diseases on my ship. Whoever looks
sturdy as an oak, with meat and muscle,

I pick right away. Whoever looks withered,
sickly, or old, I ignore like yesterday's
news. If only life were this simple.
I'm nearly finished when Chodaton
Akodé offers me a bonus.

A relative of his, a nobleman named
Gumpa. He's reportedly unparalleled
in strength and dignity. It perplexes me
why Akodé would offer up his own family.
But who am I to judge?

GUMPA
SOLD

I am not shocked when Cousin Akodé forces me into the care of this thin, bearded white man named Foster.

He and Uncle Glèlè have been looking for a way to get rid of me—because they fear me.

More and more people are starting to think like I do, and we grow in numbers to take a stand against Glèlè and his followers.

Shows you the kind of cowards they are, weeding out strong-minded people to prey on the innocent.

There are few things worse than family selling out family.

Africans selling other Africans.

I will not cry out as I am dragged away.

I am a leader, and I will not be defeated by any man.

WILLIAM
LAST NIGHT IN OUIDAH

My day's work is finished.
I alert the interpreter to have
my cargo loaded up on the *Clotilda*
by 10:00 a.m. tomorrow.
Not sure how Captain Tim will feel,

but I decide not to have them branded.
Less risk of infection. Besides, the smell
of burning flesh might inflame my allergies.
I head back to my abode for one last night.
Lots to do in the morning.

I need to get these scared monkeys
aboard the *Clotilda*. Then, home to
Alabama. They better not be surly tomorrow,
because I won't be in the mood for any
foolishness. I've got enough on my mind.

J. B.

VERTIGO

As a stowaway, I suffered from seasickness.
Now I could get smashed by a torrent of tornadoes
and it wouldn't cause me vertigo. I've survived

scurvy, dysentery, and many other maladies.
But sitting here at anchor for so many days
has got me nervous. I blame Foster—

he's taking forever to arrive with the slaves.
This journey makes me want to hurry my plans to be
my own captain. When are we going to get underway?

KOSSOLA

LAST MEAL IN AFRICA

When de men bring in plates
of palm oil and rice, dey say, "Eat up!
Tomorrow you'll be on the ship!"
Some of my brothers in bondage cry then—
especially Kupollee, whose cheeks
look as if he got caught in a rainstorm.
A sharp pain stabs my chest.
De loneliness and de not knowing what's
to become of us. De certainty that
de ship will carry us away from Africa,
from my family and my home in Bantè.
And not everyone has been chosen
by skinny little Captain Foster.
I don't want to be put apart from de ones
I've come to know in de barracoon.
Life has become one long series
of separations. At first it feels like
I'm drowning in agony, but I make
myself focus on de good. By morning
I'm ready to *swim*. Kupollee's coming.
And I've got other new friends, too—
Gumpa, of course. Oluale, who's closer
to thirty than twenty and de oldest
among us. And Ausy, a fisherman.
I'm not alone. We'll all get through it together.

WILLIAM
FIRST-CLASS TRAVEL

6:00 a.m. Sunlight's playing peekaboo
with the clouds. Now you see it,
now you don't. I ride a hammock fastened
to the heads of two of Akodé's men.
Soon I'll be back on board the *Clotilda*.

This time my cargo's waiting for me.
My body swings. My escorts' feet dig
into the rocky shore. A man could get
used to the Ouidah way of life. For one last
time, I'm a regular King Louis XIV of France.

GUMPA

OUT INTO THE DAYLIGHT

I have no family now.

I know, sure as I am chained up in this sweatbox of a shack, that each relative of mine would be captured as well if they tried to find me, because Cousin Akodé and Uncle Glèlè are in a secret war with our own people.

No one should absorb this kind of agony, or even witness it—people shriek in the night as if their bodies have been sliced open and their souls are being excavated.

At daybreak we are led out in shackles, so that we can only inch along like ducklings following their mother.

I am glad for Kossola's company as jangling chains pierce the early-morning air.

"Tell me your story," Kossola says, and he listens with the focus of one accustomed to stories and storytelling.

The way he looks at me makes me stand taller, as if I truly can lead us through this crucible.

Not all family is defined by blood.

WILLIAM

TRADE-OFFS

I've never been so glad to see my ship!
As soon as I'm safely on deck, I order
the men to release the sealed barrels.
They hold $9,000 in commodities and gold.
Chodaton Akodé's men wait in the water.

They grab each watertight container.
With payment secured, the Africans
are unshackled. Akodé's men load them onto
canoes. I wonder if they can read the word
SLAVE emblazoned upon each painted boat?

ABILẸ
WAITING OUR TURN

Kêhounco doesn't cry, only watches the canoes
      with her bright cheetah eyes. Some capsize,
spilling people who look just like us into the sea.
          One by one they disappear under the waves.

Kêhounco doesn't look away. She's just a year older,
      yet sometimes she is so much braver than me.
I stand just a little apart from her so she won't detect my tremble.
      The *Clotilda* bobs in swells that rise

like a mountain of elephants. Part of me wants to run.
      But I know they would only catch me. If we must go,
then I want it done. Kêhounco and I will not get eaten by the sea.
      We will ride the waves together.

KÊHOUNCO
CANOE MEN

The men load the canoes with bags and other people from the barracoon.

I dig my heels into the sand as they paddle out to three ships—
up-down, up-down with the waves—then come back and fill the canoes again.

When it's my turn, I don't want to go, but I've seen what they do to those who refuse.
The beach is littered with dead bodies. I want to cry for Eniọlá, for my sisters.
Everything turns fuzzy as our canoe carries us away from the shore.

GUMPA

LIVING NIGHTMARE

Most of my brothers and sisters in bondage have never seen the ocean before, so I soothe and reassure them with words.

When the white men jerk us up and throw us into a canoe, again, I offer reassurances.

SMACK! I get cracked with a wooden oar across my back.

One of the white men brings his arm up for what I am sure will be another strike, but instead he presses his finger to his lips and says, "Shush."

As they row us toward the big ship, angry waves lift the canoe into the sky, then slam us down on the water, again and again.

We rise so high I think I am going to fall backward into the ocean—once an African royal, now I am considered less than a pile of excrement.

I can do nothing to comfort my brothers and sisters now.

CLOTILDA
THE WORST

Here they come in canoes—human bodies shackled, scared, screaming.
My whole frame revolts against the anchors that hold me, but to no avail.

Oh, how sorry I am for the pain and suffering to come—for the crossing
we will share, and for what fate awaits the Africans in Alabama.

J. B.

INTRODUCTIONS

After Foster finally arrives—about time—the crew
and I strip clothes off the slaves fast as
we can. Can't have them bringing their vermin

onto this ship. They kick, shout, and squirm. "You'll get
new clothes," I say, "once we get to America!"
They keep their eyes down and cover their crotches.

KUPOLLEE

NAKED

Once
we are
all naked—
except for my
ear hoops—the crew shoves
us in the hold like meat.
I never felt so ashamed.
I look for Kossola, but he's
not on the ship. Where could my friend be?

KOSSOLA

LEFT BEHIND

I can't believe de sea! How it crashes
and rages. "What are you so angry
about?" I ask it, and pace along de shore,
daring de waves to lick my feet.
I'm so engaged that I don't realize
at first that I've wandered away from
my group. Now de beach is near empty.
"Kupollee!" He's not beside me.
He's in a boat with Ausy, Oluale,
and Gumpa, riding toward de ship.
Loneliness and fear grip me as
I splash into de waves. "Wait! Wait for me!"
There's nowhere to run without getting
caught, no family left to run to.
De ones on de boat are my family now.
But dey don't hear my words. Dey float
farther and farther away from me,
closer and closer to de *Clotilda*.
I don't want to be left alone, so I scramble
across de sand to de closest white man.
"What about me?" He scowls and spits
a stream of words I can't understand.
Next thing I know, he's pulling me toward
de last canoe. I don't need to speak
his language to know he's telling me
to hurry and get in. So that's what I do.

J. B.

THROUGH THE SPYGLASS

I can't believe we haven't set sail yet. These slaves
are the most slippery, akimbo sons of guns I've seen
in a dog's age. As soon as the captain's back is turned,

I switch out and stand watch instead. I spy two vessels
advancing toward us ten miles away. When I yell out,
the crew stops and turns on Foster, eyes ablaze.

If they capture us, we're going to get arrested for trafficking
slaves. Foster shrugs, like he's some kind of royalty.
"*Clotilda* can outrun them. Tend to your business."

I scramble into action, and the crew follows. We get
the rest of the cargo loaded in mere minutes. If I can help
get us out of this tight spot, then I'll deal with Foster.

V.

VOYAGE TO AMERICA

MAY 1860–JULY 1860

WILLIAM
ANCHORS AWEIGH

In our rush to evade capture, we leave port
missing fifteen of the 125 Africans.
Captain Tim's not going to be happy about that.
I'll try to remind him—if he'll listen—that 110 bodies
for what we paid is still an excellent deal.

Clotilda, once again, doesn't disappoint.
She skedaddles out of there barely
ahead of two impending vessels.
They can't begin to catch us.
Lord, I love this ship.

CLOTILDA

DAY ONE

I cheer on those two vessels, hoping they'll catch me and set the Africans
free. Arrest all these white men and capture Glèlè and Akodé, too.

But it doesn't happen. My burden is that once my riggings are set
and someone mans this wheel and spindle of mine, I fly!

I leave those boats behind and am out of any ship's range in four hours.
I've always thought I could handle anything—

until I hear the wails of Africans trapped belowdecks,
their souls being crushed by loneliness, fear, and abuse.

Their screams threaten to tear me apart, but their long stretches of silence
are even worse. I have the open sea to ride upon, but what must it be like

for them? I do what I can to make it a smooth crossing.
The captain and crew may not care about them, but I do.

With each surge across the waves, I fight to keep us all safe and strong.
If I'd been built with a heart, it would be broken.

KOSSOLA

DAY TWO

Dey put us in de hold, in de bottom
of de ship. Divide us into two groups:
men, and women with de children.
It's dark, so dark. All of us men pressed
skin to skin—probably twenty-five of us.
Ceiling so low only de shortest among
us can stand upright. De heat so heavy
it's like being pinned by a hippopotamus.
We don't know where we're going,
only that we're moving—
de ship lifts us and rolls us. Some faint
from de turmoil. I envy them, because at
least it gives them a few minutes of peace.
As my stomach roils, my thoughts turn
muddy. What is my name? Where am I?
I fill my mind with a picture of de Bantè
market. Bàbá àgbà and de stall
full of people smiling over de yams.
Up above, de big blue sky smiling, too.

J. B.

DAY THREE

I thought I knew what it meant to roast on a ship
until I see, clear as my hands in front of me,
fat plumes of steam rising through the grates—

courtesy of the hot, packed bodies belowdecks.
They're encased down there so tightly it's a wonder
they can even breathe. Gratitude fills my cells.

Number one: For my white skin. No one's going
to seal me up with the chattel.
Number two: It's not my job to give them water.

KOSSOLA

DAY FOUR

My throat gets so gritty down
in de hold that I can no longer speak.
When Kupollee says, "Tell me a story,"
I grunt and shake my head. "Use your
hands," he says. Doesn't matter that
it's too dark to see. De way we're squeezed
together, he can sense my movements.
When I press my fingertips and thumbs
into de shape of a circle to mean de sun's
coming up, he says, "Good, good."
When I pat my hand on my head
to represent our king, he says, "Keep
going." So I do, and it helps distract
me until de sailors come. Dey slop water
at us using a tiny wooden scoop—
a spoon, really—not even a cup.
De water tastes like vinegar, and some
spit it out. But Gumpa says in his deep voice,
"Drink. You will die if you do not drink."
De taste doesn't bother me. I'd drink
gallons of it! But no, dey snatch it away
after just a swallow. It about breaks
me open when dey move onto de next
prisoner. Even though I know everyone's
just as thirsty as me, I want it for myself.
If I still had a voice, I'd cry out. It's good
that I don't. It's good Kupollee's beside me,
asking me to tell him a story.

ABILẸ
DAY FIVE

So dark—like living in endless night.
          The only way I know it's day again
is because that's when they bring us water:
                    once in the morning, again at night.

I mark the days by singing with Kêhounco. We do
          baby counting songs: "Ọkan, èjì, ẹta, ẹrin,
àrún." She doesn't complain, not once. "Reminds me
                    of home," she says. The only time she gets

upset is in the night, when the ship rolls over
          the waves, and other women howl like hyenas.
"Only cowards howl like that," she says. But I understand
                    why they do it—it proves they're still alive.

"Part of me wants to howl, too," I confess. She stares
          at me hard, daring me to do it. Instead, I place my
hands over her ears to help block out those mournful sounds.
                    Eventually her ready-to-pounce posture softens.

Her eyelids fall, and I know by her steady breathing
          that she's asleep. She may be fierce, but she still needs
me as much as I need her. I do the only thing that helps us
                    survive—oh so softly, I sing.

KÊHOUNCO

DAY SIX

Our day starts as usual, with Abilę singing:

"Òkan, èjì, ęta, ęrin, àrún, ęfà."
Instead of bringing us water, the soldiers throw open the doors.

When rain blows in, the women chatter like gulls and lift their hands
to catch it. Abilę and I do, too—pressing our moist palms to the sky,
to our mouths. I don't even mind that most of it tastes salty, like tears.

ABILẸ
DAY SEVEN

I am too stomach-sick to sing. Kêhounco counts the numbers off
    on my fingers: "Ọkan, èjì, ẹta, èrin, àrún,
ẹfà, èje." I am too sick even to drink, but
        Kêhounco still puts her wet fingers in my mouth.

Instead of bringing me comfort, they make me gag.
    I wish I could cut my stomach away from my body.
It's like a crocodile has snapped me with his jaws,
      and for hours I almost pray for my life

to be over. But then I chase that thought away
    and focus on Kêhounco. She strokes my forehead
and cheeks. "You will be okay, sister. You will be okay."
      The world may not need me, but Kêhounco does.

KUPOLLEE

DAY EIGHT

Ship
full of
sickness, hold
sour with vomit.
My back weeps like fresh
fruit from rubbing against
the planks. Even Kossola
moans about wet sores on his wrists
and ankles. Our shackles heavy, cold.

GUMPA

DAY NINE

We have gone from a dark, scorching enclosure on land, to a canoe nearly drowning in the roiling seas, to a dusky, searing jail on a ship at war with the ocean.

Tempests hit us so hard you can hear skulls cracking against metal as bodies smash into each other.

"It cannot last forever," I tell them. "We must hang on, show them our power."

My once-mighty frame shrinks from dehydration and lack of food.

What is left of my skin is mountainous with bruises.

What I would not give for a sliver of sunlight!

I think back to when I was a boy, running down dusty roads, my mother and father watching over me.

My eyes grow damp as I recall the warmth of their embrace.

KÊHOUNCO

DAY TEN

I can hardly hear Abilẹ̀'s song.

The sea shouts, and the *Clotilda* answers. Even growing up
in a house full of sisters, I have never heard a worse argument.

"Ọ̀kan, èjì, ẹ̀ta, ẹ̀rin, àrún, ẹ̀fà, èje, ẹ̀jọ, ẹ̀sán, ẹ̀wá," I sing,
counting off the numbers on Abilẹ̀'s fingers. The world fights
outside, and we fight for our lives inside this seaswept prison.

KUPOLLEE

DAY ELEVEN

We
shrivel
like beans in
drought. Our stalks bend,
nearly snap, as huge
waves lift us to the sky,
then drop us to the bottom
of the sea. We are inside a
terrible story. When will it end?

WILLIAM

DAY TWELVE

Clotilda is moving at a good clip.
Operating at six knots.
I would let these Africans up
for a blast of fresh air, but if I did,
I'd risk us being spotted.

I'm about to go over my midday review
of the ship's log when a sense of
foreboding washes over me.
It won't disappear no matter how
I try to chase it away with maps and charts.

Maybe tomorrow I will allow
the slaves to visit the top deck.
I search the star-speckled sky
for a shooter to wish on and ward off
any ill luck. Here's hoping.

KOSSOLA

DAY THIRTEEN

No one's more surprised than me
when de sailors come in and say,
"Get up! Get up!" Dey drag us to our
feet and march us upstairs to de deck.
Not everyone's well enough to walk
after being crammed on de floor
for so long. Those invalid prisoners
get carried up de steps as de crew
swears and screws up their faces
at de foul odors and filth. What do dey
expect, leaving us down here
to mess ourselves? I don't know
what to think when we get to de top.
I grip de railing and look out, searching
for signs of land. But there's nothing
but sky and more sky. Sea and more sea.
My stomach swims. Where are we?
Where are we going? "How will we
ever get back?" I ask Gumpa. "How
will we know de way home?"
Gumpa's voice comes, rumbly as ever.
"We will know." Beside me, Kupollee's
eyes are shiny. He presses his palm
against his chest, just over his heart.
"Like a seed knows to stretch
toward light," he says. "The map
is inside us." I nod, and my eyes
fall on Abilè from across de deck.

"You're alive!" I say, smiling, and she
smiles back. De girl beside her stares
me down, her body all hunt and muscle.
"Ǹlẹ́ o," I say. Hello. So she knows
I intend no harm. Abilẹ̀ strokes de girl's
cheek. "This is Kêhounco, my cheetah-sister."
Abilẹ̀'s de one to tell me their ages.
Images rush into my mind of when I was
fifteen, sixteen—my soldier training.
My dreams of orò. And here dey are
holding one another up. "You take
good care of each other," I say.
Kêhounco shrugs. "It's what sisters do."
I talk to as many people as I can that day—
so happy to be alive!
De fresh sea air, all that sunshine
makes me forget just for a time
that we're prisoners. But de crew
is quick to remind us with their whips.

WILLIAM
IMMIGRANT LULLABY

Clotilda is slowly rocking on the swells
as dark indigo skies caress us. I lift
my pipe so I can knock back a nip of brandy.
What a peaceful evening—except for
the sounds coming from belowdecks.

It's in a language I don't understand,
yet I can hear the brokenness of their voices:
altos, contraltos, baritones, basso
profundos singing symphonies
of hope, despite their pain.

The voices pierce the air and very
nearly puncture my heart. My parents
have shared with me songs like this—songs
they learned when traveling from England
to Nova Scotia. The same songs were ringing

in the night when I traveled from Nova Scotia
to America. And now I hear them again, only
in a different language, as the slaves journey
to Mobile. I tamp down my feelings.
I can't think of them as humans. I won't.

KUPOLLEE

DREAMS

Dreams
come when
I wish they
wouldn't. It hurts
to wake with visions
of family, gardens,
and òrìṣà traditions
so vivid when I'm shackled, soiled.
Anger swells, rescues me from drowning.

KOSSOLA

BROTHERHOOD

As de days pass, we fall into a new
routine of daily walks on de deck.
De best part's how it allows us
to talk to one another, to share
stories of home, stories of capture.
Kupollee watches de water,
looking for change. "Guava-green
today," he says, after days
of blue. None of us knows what
de changing colors mean, but each
day we search for land.
"Can't stay on this ship forever,"
Ausy says. There's so much
we don't know. And yet we're in it
together, like back when I was
training for orò. My initiation
ceremony seems like it happened
in a different lifetime. But de affection
I feel for Kupollee, Ausy,
and de other men is much
de same—a sense of brotherhood,
like we know de same secrets.
De sailors may have stripped
and chained us, left us in de hold
for weeks, but we're still breathing.
We're all warriors and survivors.

ABILÈ
A DIFFERENT KIND OF FAMILY

When Kossola tells me about his parents and Adérónkẹ́,
     part of me wants to tell him about my family.
But then I remember my promise to myself,
        the one I made when I placed the stone on the pile.

"It doesn't matter," I tell him. "I am here now.
     You, us, Kêhounco—this is my family now."
He nods, but there's a glint in his eye. "Someday
        you'll tell me," he says. "I won't give up."

I hold his gaze. The new me is not ashamed of my nakedness.
     The new me knows the decision to tell him my story
or not is my choice, and mine alone. As words swirl away
        on the wind, I am filled with a strange stillness.

We have different religions, different languages.
     But because we're trapped together on the *Clotilda*,
we're linked by invisible threads. Not just by what
        we say. Also by what we don't say.

KÊHOUNCO

THE WATCHER

Abilè calls me her cheetah-sister, but Kossola calls me "de watcher."

Growing up with a houseful of sisters taught me words matter less than what I can learn with my eyes and ears. On board *Clotilda*, I listen and watch the crew.

I know things are going well when the sailors slap each other on the back. As they lift the sails, I can tell their moods by how quickly they draw the ropes. When the captain scowls at the sky, I know that somewhere a storm is brewing.

KUPOLLEE
THE LANGUAGE OF WATER

When
green seas
blossom red,
I'm certain we
will either die on
this ship or run aground.
Kêhounco is first to spy
land. She points, then spits a small shell
into her palm, clasps it to her heart.

KÊHOUNCO

DAY 20

On the day our count comes to "ogún" for twenty days at sea, the captain frowns.

He climbs the mast, checks his spyglass again and again. He stays up
there for a while, then rushes back down. As he shouts instructions,

the crew lowers the sail, drops anchor. I grab Abilẹ̀'s arm as he orders
us back into the hold. "Down," he says. "Now!" We are mostly silent
as the *Clotilda* bobs in place all night, doesn't move again until morning.

CLOTILDA
TEN FEET FROM GLORY

I'm a wooden hulk of frustration. On June 30, while cruising toward
the Bahamas, I sight a buried ship directly in our path.

I stay calm, hopeful. Could this be my opportunity to free the Africans
in my hold, release them from their captivity? If only I could guarantee

they wouldn't drown. Not that it matters. That blasted Foster—he's
many despicable things, but the man sure can steer a ship.

He spots the wreck with his spyglass, then orders the crew to anchor me
not ten feet away from the submerged steamer.

Oh, to be so close to collision, shipwreck, SOS! Had marine patrols
arrived, the Africans would have been discovered and taken to land.

Since the Bahamas outlawed slavery in 1834, Foster and the crew
would be arrested, and the Africans freed. So close, I say. But not close enough.

WILLIAM

TENACITY

From the first flare of sunlight
through the dark, moonlit hours,
there's one fresh problem after another.
I hardly get a moment's peace.
Every cell in my body screams for rest.

Today, while sailing near Tortuga,
Northrop catches sight of two more men-of-war.
"Take down the fore-topmast and square sail,"
I order my men. Our ship now looks as
innocent as a milk-drinking virgin.

KUPOLLEE

LAND, HO!

The day the sea changes to turquoise,
I know we must be close to land.
When Captain Foster orders
us immediately
belowdecks, I'm sure.
"Almost over,
Kossola."
We link
hands.

WILLIAM

DETAILS AND PLANNING

I've been planning with Captain
Tim for months before leaving
Mobile about what happens when
I arrive back home. First, unload the cargo.
Second, give each crew member

their wages. Third, head to a
Mexican port called Tampico.
Fourth, have the *Clotilda* undergo
one last retrofitting to revert it
to an unassuming shipping schooner.

Fifth, christen her with a new name
before she sails off to New Orleans
with a freight of edibles and clapboard
homes. It'll be like her former life
as a slave ship never existed.

The name *Clotilda* will disappear—
a phantom in the night. I take
pride knowing her body and soul
will be sailing on, moving fast as migratory
whales for many years to come.

GUMPA
WAITING

Moans fill the hold as I swab my parched tongue across swollen,
chapped lips that are now ragged as mountain ridges.

Beside me, Oluale and Jaba—who has not spoken since our
capture—tremble like trees in a windstorm.

As I place my hands over theirs, my throat erupts in agony. I croak
out the word "water" to the white man.

When he gets to me, I crook my head toward my friends so that he
will give them a drink first.

It is satisfying to watch them guzzle the water.

When it is my turn, the white man shakes his head and spits in my
face, barking words I interpret as "There is your water."

Oluale and Jaba lean their heads against my shoulders after the
white man is gone.

When they look up and try to mouth the words "Mo dúpẹ́,"
I shush them, then lightly press my forehead against both
of theirs.

J. B.

SIGNALS

Hello, Gulf of Mexico. Normally this is the time
during a sail when I start feeling sad for the journey
to be over. But with these slaves on board

I can't wait to disembark. I'm weary of hiding among
these islands when we're so close to port.
Goodness, those slaves sure can make a racket.

Foster orders the crew to go belowdecks to shut them up.
After they've been lashed, I snag some green branches
I cut earlier on land, go below, and scatter them around.

I'm not sure the Africans are smart enough to know what
I'm trying to tell them: We're getting close to our arrival.
They surprise me by quieting down. Finally.

KOSSOLA

ARRIVAL

After de sailors tease us with de green
branches promising we'll soon be landing,
de ship doesn't move for hours.
"Why are dey waiting?" I ask Kupollee
again and again. "Soon this will be over,"
he says. "We'll get off this ship."
I don't have to see his teeth with
their chipped-out V to know he's smiling.
I can hear it in his voice. That's when
termites swarm my stomach. "What will
happen to us next? Where are dey taking us?"
"Shhh," Kupollee says. "Rest now."
I try, but my orò-trained body stays alert
to every sound and movement.
I can't wait to leave de *Clotilda*
behind for good.

VI.

MOBILE SWAMPLANDS
JULY 1860

CLOTILDA
ENTRANCE POINT

As I sail through the Mississippi Sound and temporarily settle in Grand Bay,
I thank the moon, tides, and stars. I would not have made it without

their songs ringing into the briny air, helping push me forward.
Their trials and tribulations in America are just beginning,

but at least I will be relieved of this burden—
and their feet will again know solid ground.

WILLIAM
SURPRISE

Instead of arriving onshore to find
Captain Tim's smiling face, followed
by a firm handshake and a clap on the
back for all my hard work and loyalty,
he's not there. After all our plans! *Where is he?*

"Where's our money?" Northrop shouts.
"You told us we'd get our pay as soon
as we dropped anchor." He lunges at me like
a tiger after its prey. I lift my hands in
surrender. "It's a misunderstanding.

Captain Tim will be here. I promise."
Northrop glares, then spits at my boots.
"You better be right, Foster. Or else."
When I promise to go ashore to get the
money from Captain Tim, he says,

"If we don't receive payment, we will
find you, and we will kill you." The fire
in his eyes tells me that he means business.
I rally off more promises and hop into my canoe,
praying I can outsmart them one more time.

CLOTILDA
STATE OF EXCITEMENT

My wooden frame shimmies in elation as Foster rows away so ferociously I imagine his arms will dislodge from their sockets.

Belowdecks the Africans huddle and shudder like sails in a gale. *Soon,* I want to whisper to them. *Soon you'll be free of me.*

We're anchored and exposed. Perhaps sailors on another vessel will discover us before Foster returns and end this madness once and for all.

TIMOTHY
SUNDAY MORNING ARRIVAL

Finally, a day off! Nothing like a Sunday morning
after putting in another ninety-six-hour work week.
I prop my boots and inhale some fine tobacco out of my pipe.
"Noah," I call to my favorite slave. "Pour me a whiskey neat."
As he limps over, I unwind like a weary clock. When horse hooves
tear up Telegraph Road, it can only mean one thing.

I meet the messenger at the door. He doesn't even dismount,
just leans down, cups his hand over my ear.
"Your shipment arrived, sir." I give him a wink, then nod at Noah.
"Boy, get me my horses right now." It's time to hunt down
Hollingsworth, best tugboat commander south of the Mason-Dixon Line.

I bring James, my brother Burns's slave, with me—because
a man should always bring along some help. He's young and strong,
keeps his trap shut, and he's got a good head on his shoulders,
even if he does wear those strange braids.
A fine, obedient, healthy piece of chattel. I would take Noah,
but his limp makes him better served on my property only.
As James and I ride toward Mobile, it may look like I'm as cool
as the air after an October rainstorm, but inside my heart is
exploding like fireworks on the Fourth of July.

JAMES

ST. JOHN'S CHURCH

As we ride away
Master Timothy says, "Boy,
I'll bet two jugs of
moonshine Hollingsworth's at church."
Sure enough, when we arrive,

there he is, kneeling,
his head bent in prayer. Master
Timothy barges
in with all the grace of a
runaway bull. Bowed heads snap

in his direction.
He taps Hollingsworth's arm, leads
him around to where
I wait. "I've got a ship that
must be hauled right now, my friend.

I only trust you
to do it right. Plus, it's good
money." When Master
Timothy lets him know how
much, Hollingsworth shows his teeth.

"Well," he says. "I think
the good Lord will understand."
After they shake hands,
Master Timothy smiles, looks
up, offers a quick "Amen."

TIMOTHY

THE ELABORATE SCHEME

On board Hollingsworth's tugboat the *Billy Jones*, I crane
my head hoping, praying no other ships are out here to witness
us drag the *Clotilda* to a hiding place to transfer the slaves.
As the *Clotilda* comes into sight, my heart pounds like high tide
on a rocky Maine shore. There she is!

In order to get things started on the right foot with Foster
and the crew—who might very well be unruly after so long
at sea—I greet them by holding up a bag of coins.
Nothing like a little jingle to encourage a bit more cooperation.
I know my strategy has worked when the weathered sailors
get busy hooking the ship to the tugboat.

Foster, meanwhile, glares at me with a look that says
he'd like to punch my pilot lights out. "Just a little longer,"
I promise. Burns is waiting for us just below
the mouth of the Spanish River, where we'll transfer
the slaves from the *Clotilda* to the *Czar*.
It's a miracle we haven't been spotted by
port authorities and customs already.
I clap his back. "It's sure good to see you, Foster.
Have I ever steered you wrong?"

KÊHOUNCO
MYSTERY SOUNDS

To pass the time, I roll my shell around in my mouth, and Abilè and I play games.

When the ship jolts suddenly, like something's run into it,
she says, "A rhino thinks our ship is another rhino, and it's charging us."

When we hear a loud buzz, and then the boat begins to move,
I say, "Bees. Angry bees." Even though neither of us has ever heard
so many bees at once. What will happen to us next?

CLOTILDA
NOTHING LEFT TO GIVE

My weary structure is hitched to the *Billy Jones* and dragged up
the Spanish River. I'm grateful to have someone else do the sailing

for a change. We turn and enter the opening of the Mobile River before
reaching Twelve Mile Island. It's nothing more than wilderness—

private and secluded. The *Czar* waits to relieve me of the Africans. I wonder
if they realize they are simply moving from one nightmare to another.

As for me, my future is no less certain. Meaher and Foster have nowhere
to hide me, and no way to get me to the Pánuco River in Mexico, where

I was to be cleaned and refitted. I shudder when I hear Meaher say the word
"burn." Is that really to be my fate?

"No," Foster says. "Not the *Clotilda*! She's such a great ship."
"There isn't time!" Meaher says. "Patrols are everywhere."

Foster is no match for Meaher's logic. He turns silent, no doubt as exhausted
as I am after this arduous journey. And so I shall drown in flames.

ABILẸ
LANDFALL

When the sailors open the hold to let us out,
      I run my hand along the scratches I've made
to mark the days. Ogójì. "Ogójì," Kêhounco confirms.
          We've been on the *Clotilda* for forty days.

My legs tremble as we climb the stairs. What will we see?
      For a moment the ghosts I left behind swirl around me,
but I push them back. They are of no use to me here.
         They would only weigh me down.

I reach for Kêhounco's hand, for what's real. Her fingers
      are warm in mine, even though now we can't offer
each other much more than bones. Whatever fate awaits us,
        we will face it together. Just as we have done all along.

KUPOLLEE
NEW VIEW

Night
skies give
way to dawn—
surrounded by
land, not sea! I suck
in fresh air. Kossola
claps my back. "We're here," he says,
grinning. "Yes," I say, feeling my
legs grow brawny as the strange, tall trees.

KOSSOLA

AN END AND A BEGINNING

As de heavy air moves in and out
of my lungs, I can't stop de joy
from spreading across my face.
After so many days of ocean,
we see on both sides of de ship
acres of thick, leafy trees I can't
name. No dusty hills, no buildings,
no people anywhere. Beneath us
de river rolls clean and green.
I don't know what's coming around
de next riverbend, can't imagine
what this new life will bring.
But it can't be worse than what
we've already experienced.
It can't be.

ABILẸ
WALKING THE PLANK

When the sailors ready a plank, I am sure
    my feet will finally again touch land.
But that is not what happens. Instead, they
       attach the plank to another boat—

the *Czar*, it says on the side. I don't know how to say it
    or what it means. But I do know one thing:
I am not getting on another boat. "No." I shake my head.
      "No, no, no." I shrink back

as the other prisoners move past me. "It's okay,"
    Kêhounco says and strokes my cheek—as if
I am a child. "They might cook us and eat us," I say, my
      belly full of knots. Kossola, listening, shakes his head.

"Dey won't eat you, Abilẹ," he says. "You're too tough."
    I slap at him, and it loosens something inside
me. "Come on," Kêhounco urges. I take one step,
      then another, my feet strengthened by friendship.

WILLIAM
FINAL VOYAGE

With the slaves now transferred
from one ship to another, I ascend
back to the *Clotilda*. I assess
her various intact and battered sections.
Filthy floorboards on the lowest level.

The many empty kegs in the hold.
All the riggings and sails I crafted
with my own hands. So many trials,
and still this ship sailed ever onward.
Guilt rises in my gut.

I made this fine schooner a slave ship,
befouling it with bodily waste and fluids.
While navigating her away from the *Czar*
I stare at the stars, preparing my heart
to bring my favorite ship to its final act.

KÊHOUNCO
THE WAYS OF WHITE MEN

They don't eat us, but they do lock us up—again.

I watch as Captain Foster greets the new crew. They do not bow to him, only shake hands as equals. He's not as powerful as I first thought.

Every interaction, whether shake or embrace, is quick. Their eyes are shifty, too. They are not honest men. Things go better for all of us when we, too, move fast. Which means I truly must practice being a cheetah, like Abilẹ says.

WILLIAM
ONE LAST LOOK

First, I drop anchor at the back side
of Twelve Mile Island in a place
called Bayou Canot. Second, I rush
to my cabin, remove my desk, chair,
and clock from the *Clotilda*.

At least I'll have these keepsakes.
Third, I arrange the hull with
seven cords of pine fatwood,
kindle each one, then hurry down
the plank, shaking with sadness.

When I turn around, the flames are
already climbing. Fury swells inside me
thick and hot as an Alabama summer.
A chunk of my spirit disappears
like smoke as my ship incinerates.

Captain Tim said we had to
burn the evidence of our crime.
But wasn't there another way?
Clotilda, you're worth more than
any abundance of black bodies.

CLOTILDA
NEVER FORGOTTEN

After sixteen weeks of horror, the flames lick and roar.
Part of me welcomes the heat.

My oak and pine planks sputter, crackle.
By some miracle my hull sinks before it burns completely.

Part of me remains lodged in the channel—
a confession buried by water, waiting for someone to release me.

TIMOTHY
TAKING STOCK

Now that I've got the Africans and the *Clotilda* crew
on board the *Czar*, I order Burns to double-check
to make sure all our decoys are in place in case
the authorities give us any problems.
It must appear as if we're on a routine shipping voyage.

Soon we are underway. As we cruise the Tombigbee's
rich waters en route to my friend John Dabney's
plantation, I take stock of what's happened so far.
I hate that we had to burn the *Clotilda*, but it couldn't
be helped. It's the cost of doing business.
And also to avoid being jailed for breaking the law.

My chess pieces are lining up well—
only a couple more to put in place.
Soon I'll not only have a whole new batch
of slaves to strengthen our labor force,
but also a tidy profit
after I sell some of them off.

Here's hoping for smooth sailing ahead.

KOSSOLA

ON SOLID GROUND

Not more than a few hours pass
before dey stop de boat. This time
when dey march us up and out,
there's no other ship for us to board—
only land. When my bare toes touch
de grassy clearing, I cry out and dig
my heels in de dirt. Solid earth,
after so long on de ship! My body's
soft, wobbly, and thin as de canebrake
that surrounds us. I'd like to sit
awhile, breathe it in. But there's
no time for that. De one dey call James
takes charge of us. His skin is dark,
but not as dark as ours, and he says
"yessir" every time de white men speak
to him. I like de way his hair hangs
in neat braids. He must be a slave.
Naked and filthy as I am, I can't bear
to look him in de eye, but I watch him
closely for clues about how to behave
in this new world.

JAMES

FIRST MEETING

These Africans are
lost as stray puppies running
in a thunderstorm.
Each one has skin the color
of dark coffee, blacker than

anything I've seen
in my twenty years on earth.
They shuffle along,
hunched over; their backs are a
maze of scars. I try to feed

them sausages with
hoe cakes, but these new flavors
cause some of them to
vomit. "Go slow," I say. I
point at my heart. "I'm your friend."

I take two deep breaths.
All of them look so outraged,
I don't know if they're
going to attack me or
not. I rub my two lengthy

braids repeatedly—
I do this when I'm nervous.
I've known fear like theirs,
from when I was sold with my
aunt Amy back in Charleston

and ended up here.
I'm only better off than
the Africans by
a hairsbreadth. It sure helps to
know plantation rules. Trust me.

TIMOTHY

THE ORIGINAL FLIMFLAMMER

On deck of the *Czar*, Northrop, who's nothing more than second mate,
is about foaming at the mouth. "Where's our money?" he spits.
The *Clotilda* crew behind him moans about not getting their pay yet.
I have seen a lot of unsavory men in my day, but some of these folks
make the hair on the back of my neck stand up.

"Gentlemen," I say, "I assure you with every shred of my being
that you will get your money as soon as we reach Mobile.
And—" I hold up my hand as my mind searches for just
the right enticement. "Unlimited whiskey and gambling
for each of you." As smiles lift their beards, I know I'm in the clear.
Nothing like free, unlimited alcohol to quell the anger
of some salty dogs. I dare offer one more instruction. "Only
catch is you must not be seen by either the authorities
or any of my routine passengers. You must remain hidden
for this last leg of the journey."

They grumble, but I would, too. No one loves dry land
more than a sailor returning from sea. And yet, they comply.
One by one they board the *Roger B. Taney* under cover of darkness.

KOSSOLA

DE GIFT OF CLOTHING

As soon as we're hidden in de trees,
James dumps out sacks of rags.
"Put these on," he says, motioning
for us to get dressed. He stares
at my chipped teeth but doesn't
address me. I snatch up
some garments. Doesn't matter
that de fabric is thin and scratchy.
When I pull up de pants and get
de shirt over my back, I press back tears.
Finally, some privacy, after so long
without. It's easier to talk with de women
once this basic decency has been
restored. When my eyes lock with
Abilè's, she holds my gaze, and her
lips almost curve into a smile—almost.
I'm not sorry to hear de *Czar* pull away
from de shore. We've survived so much.
We've made it to shore. Maybe it's
unwise, but I'm filled with hope—
safe in my new clothes
and ready to greet my future.

TIMOTHY

TRANSFER

Once the crew is safely tucked into the nooks and crannies
of the *Roger B. Taney*, I hightail it to dinner.
I offer a fusillade of apologies for the delay of departure,
blaming an under-the-weather chef. According to
my registered logs, this ship was scheduled to be
out of port and on its way to Montgomery hours ago.
"What were all those clanging sounds I heard earlier?"
one of my curious passengers asks.
I can't very well tell him it was a bunch of criminals,
so I answer the question with one of my own.
"What business do you have in Montgomery?"
If I know one thing to be true: When in doubt,
ask people about themselves, and they'll never
shut up. It doesn't take even two minutes for my
tardiness to be forgotten.
I'm telling you, they don't suspect a thing.

J. B.
WAGES

We've come this far, so of course we all hide
as instructed before Foster delivers us to a mail train
to make our escape. It shouldn't come as any surprise

that Foster doesn't hand off our pay until just
before our train pulls out, heading north.
I take one glance inside the envelope—

I've been bamboozled one last time! Only $700
when Foster promised to double our pay.
I've never in my life felt more like a white slave

than how I've been treated by Foster—what a low-down
excuse for a man. I toiled on a slave ship and now
have nothing to show for it except trust shattered

like glass in a hurricane. What a holy mess.
When I become captain of my own ship, I vow to never
treat another person the way I've been treated.

KUPOLLEE
IN THE SWAMP OF DESPAIR

Wild
landscape.
Watery
maze of bamboo,
bog, and mosquitoes
buzzing, biting. Snakes, fleas,
lice—all of us sick, itching.
No rain, only sweat trickling down
my back. When will the misery end?

JAMES

HIDING OUT

Master Timothy
barks out, "Take 'em, James," so for
eleven days we
move from one swamp to the next
like frogs jumping lily pads.

I'm scared we'll get caught
by the authorities. Each
African beds down
on damp, jagged ground each night.
I rely on hand signals

to convince them to
keep their loud whispers gentle
as summer clouds. I
do notice this young woman
in rags who strides straighter than

a walking stick. Her
face brightens like daybreak when
our eyes meet. I smile,
look down, then strain my ears till
I hear her name . . . Kêhounco.

TIMOTHY

FAME

I'm shoveling down some scrambled eggs with breakfast ham
while reading the paper when an article jumps out at me
with the stealth of a water moccasin.

It talks about how the *Clotilda* took the slaves to Mobile without
the authorities' knowledge and is congratulating whoever arranged
for this to happen. Which of my "friends," I wonder, couldn't keep
their mouth shut?

I read the article again, my heart leaping like a fresh-caught catfish.
Should've known the rumor mill wouldn't be able to resist going
to the newspaper. The kidnapping story has traveled
even as far as New York after being mentioned in *Harper's Weekly*.

On one hand, I'm not a fan of the rumor mill spreading my business.
Why can't society keep their traps shut about other people's affairs?

On the other hand—sweet mother of mercy—I'm famous!
This shipment of human cargo is now an open secret, right up there with
whites who impregnate their slaves, then deny the mulatto children
as their own when everyone knows different.

So much for discretion.

Mary is probably worried I'm going to get caught.
She worries about every little thing. I could cough and she'd
think I'm on my deathbed. But I'm safe from the government.
They have zero proof.

KOSSOLA

A STORY OF SILENCE

"Shhh," dey hiss at us, clamping their
hands over our mouths. It makes me
want to shout! How long can dey hide us?
How long? Finally I risk a whisper to Kupollee.
"Tell us a story," he says, "like you
did in the dark on the ship." He means
for me to use my hands to show de words
instead of speaking. So I share a story
about my family, and it's as if my parents
and siblings are beside me. I clasp
my hands and pull them to
my chest, making de sign for "home."
I wiggle my fingers to show us marching,
swimming back home. Everyone seems
to like that story—except Abilẹ. Whenever
I talk or make signs about home, she turns
away. When I'm done, my family's faces
disappear like smoke. My heart throbs
with de weight of missing them.

TIMOTHY

ARREST

I've been indicted for "improperly
bringing Negroes into America."

Thanks to people who can't mind their own business,
the representatives at both the US District Court
and the Customs House found out about the
Clotilda and the Africans. The grand jury wants to know exactly
where I was on July 7th, at the time of the alleged crime.

In my testimony I swear under oath that I was aboard
my ship the *Roger B. Taney* during the night in question,
which is true. A person can't be in two places at once,
can they? I did commit a sin of omission by not mentioning
that the Africans were on another one of my ships being
transferred to the canebrakes, but what's one little
missing fact in the grand scheme of life?

I hurry home as soon as the court frees me on bond.
Mary meets me on the porch, her cheeks wet with tears.
She's been extra emotional since becoming pregnant.
"Honey," I say, "don't you worry. When the trial comes around,
I'll have more tricks up my sleeve than a magician.
William G. Jones is likely to be a judge
on this case, and you know we're such good friends
that I named one of my vessels after him."
That seems to quell her tears.

I found me a good woman.

MARY

A WIFE'S WORRY

I know what Timothy has done.
His actions affect our unborn child,
yet he acts as if it's all for fun.
What else has Timothy done?
I'm his wife, but part of me is tempted to run—
If only his ambitions were less reckless, less wild.
I don't approve of what Timothy has done.
His actions affect me and our unborn child.

TIMOTHY
ONE STEP AHEAD

Even though Judge Jones—a compatriot of the highest order—
is sure to be on my side, the government sticks to my tail
like a swarm of gnats. Federal prosecutors also try to nab
my pal Dabney and my brother Burns for supposedly housing
fresh Africans on their property.

Someone who shall remain nameless—because I don't gossip
like the rest of Mobile high society—tips me off about the US Marshal
authorizing the use of the *Eclipse* to search canebrakes and various
backwater channels to find them.

After learning from my source the date and time of their aquatic
expedition, I send the *Roger B. Taney* to move the slaves from
site to site on my family's waterfront acreage.
All this subterfuge is taking me away from my business *and* my family.
It's getting tiresome. Besides, mosquitoes are a concern.
Infections and such could be rampant. Those slaves
better not die on me. They're worth at least $700 apiece.

ABILẸ

NO COMPLAINTS

This time none of us complains about getting back
      on a boat when it means relief from the constant
attack of mosquitoes. Poor Kêhounco is nothing
          more than a giant welt.

When I try to soothe her, she pushes my hands away.
      "They knew we were getting eaten," I tell her.
"That's why they're moving us." We are worth
          more to them alive and healthy.

As the boat chugs down the river, I turn my mind
      to anything besides the itching. If only
I had some thick mud to slather on my skin! But even
          that thought is useless. Since

Kêhounco's eyes are nearly swollen shut, I try
      to watch the world the way she does. Gumpa's
shoulders are strong and solid as ever. Kossola
          smiles at something Kupollee says.

I shake my head. How is it that he can always find a smile?
      It seems like we've been in this country forever,
and yet we still haven't landed, not really. Seeing Kossola's
          shining face, I almost believe we will survive.

KÊHOUNCO
WHY I DON'T LIKE MOSQUITOES

When the white men march us off the boat, I hope we will be put in a proper house.

Instead, they shove us under a shed, to hide us during the dark hours. My skin screams every time anyone touches me. I don't know if I can bear it.

Somehow I do. When they move us back to the swamp at sunrise, they say "Shoo, shoo," as if we are goats. Abilè's eyes get wet. "I'm so sorry, my cheetah-sister." She slaps at the mosquitoes, but still they find me.

KOSSOLA

ON DE BRIGHT SIDE

It's not just mosquitoes that torment us
these nights under de shed and days
in de swamp. As de time passes,
and our situation doesn't change, we sink
into a fog of depression, a pit of not-knowing.
"This is no kind of life," Abilẹ says.
"This is not living." She's right, but I don't see
any point in thinking of it like that.
"It's only for now," I say. "Not forever.
Someday we'll go back home, I promise you
that." I help her doctor Kêhounco's bites.
We gather handfuls of dirt and spit into it,
making a kind of paste. It gives her relief,
at least until de mud dries and flakes. Then
we do it all over again. "Look," I say, trying
to cheer everyone. "These clothes dey gave us
provide some protection. We aren't naked,
and we aren't stuck in darkness, being knocked
around by de ocean." I stomp my foot.
"De ground is solid. And dey haven't eaten us."
Oluale and some others nod their heads
and agree with me, but not Abilẹ. "They
haven't eaten us *yet*," she says. But there's
a tiny smile in her voice—enough
to makẹ sunshine beam right out of my heart.

KUPOLLEE

IDLE TIME

Strange,
these days.
"Why don't we
work?" Abilè
asks. "Least we have clothes,"
Kossola says. "We must
not let them take our spirits,"
Gumpa says. "Let us remain calm."
I whisper, "We must learn their language."

TIMOTHY

IMPATIENCE

I've waited long enough for the dust to settle—it's time
to get on with the sale. When I announce the date
and place, a neighbor whom I thought for sure
I could count on backs out. "Can't be a part of this," he says.
"Just don't need to be mixed up in this business, not with
the law on your tail."

And he's not the only one who reneges. What a bunch
of poltroons! They've got no dash-fire in their souls.
Thank goodness for a few real men who know the secret
to being successful is a willingness to take risks.

Let's get down to business.

JAMES
UNWILLING PARTICIPANT

As I'm guiding these
white men by boat to where the
auction will happen,
I wonder if the slave who
captained the boat to where I

was sold as a boy
had the same feeling I have
now of being stuck
in a wire snare with nowhere
to go. I swallow my pain.

GUMPA

ROUTINE MORNING

The sky in this place stays smothered in a silvery shield of gray.

Each morning we are guided from the shanty to the swamp, our bodies emanating sheets of perspiration due to the scorching heat.

The white men and the black man called James must not think us intelligent enough to learn their words, because whenever they want us to take a seat or to shut up, they gesture with their hands, make clicking sounds with their tongues and shooing sounds with their breath.

On this day a hot wind pushes through the air, and I am filled with unease.

When I see a pack of white men walk through the high swaths of grass smoking tobacco, my heart is pierced with the precision and speed of a spear.

KOSSOLA
BACK TO BANTÈ

When dey separate us into two
chained rows—me and de other men
on one side, and Kêhounco, Abilè,
and de other women across from us—
my mind flashes to Ouidah. "No," I say,
only loud enough for Kupollee to hear.
De gawking and poking are bad enough,
but my heart clutches at de thought
of them separating us from one another.
We've been through so much together—
we're bound by de barracoon
and by de *Clotilda*. Dey can't split
us apart now. But dey can, and dey do.
As dey begin their inspections, I force
my mind back to Bantè—to when
I was a child climbing trees with Adérónké.
Dey might touch my body, but dey
can't reach any other part of me
when I'm up in that tree.

KUPOLLEE

INSPECTION

I catalog sounds as their mouths move.
I learn the word "teeth" when they force
my jaw open, press against
my chipped òrìṣà V.
I learn the word "ear"
when they finger
my gold hoops.
I don't
speak.

ABILẸ

MY MISTAKE

When the white men yank away Kossola's
        clothing, I wince. When they wave their
arms, indicating that we should all strip,
            I throw my arms around Kêhounco.

They can't take her clothes. Not with the way
        the mosquitoes make a feast of her! When Gumpa
hisses, I know I've made a terrible mistake. He has more
          experience dealing with authority figures.

One of the white men tugs a coil of leather
        from his belt—a coil of leather that becomes
a sleek black whip whistling through the air—*zzznnggg*,
          until SLICE!

The whip strikes my right shoulder, knocking me
        to the ground. When Kêhounco reaches to help
me up, I shake my head at her. I will not allow
          her to know this bite, too.

KOSSOLA

SPLIT

I squeeze my eyes shut so I don't have
to witness de whip cutting Abilè's skin.
De sound alone is enough to split open
my heart. And when it is over, and I dare
to crack open my eyelids, her body lies
crumpled in de dirt. Blood rises, making
one long stripe across her shoulders.
I am frozen as she pulls herself to standing,
and de white men begin chattering, making
their selections. Dey take turns, each
one pointing a finger at de one dey want.
You're mine, their blotchy faces say.
You come with me. A new awareness
grips my chest with de force of an anaconda.
All de time in de barracoon and on de ship
I knew we were kidnapped, yes. Prisoners
taken from Africa. But I didn't fully realize
until this moment de truth of our situation.
I don't need an interpreter to understand
we are being flat-out sold: Now we are slaves.
I have no smile for anybody on this day.

TIMOTHY

THE SALE

As the cargo's being farmed out to different owners,
I'm already counting the funds that will soon be in my pocket.
Doesn't concern me too much when the chattel gets
a little rowdy with us. It's nothing we can't handle
with a little light aggression.

Out of all the slaves, I have the most: thirty-two,
with an even split of males and females, not to mention
a man—yes, a man—with gold hoop earrings. There's one
of them who stares daggers at me. Always has his head up,
shoulders rolled back—everyone seems to look to him for guidance.
If he ever gets out of hand, I'll have to be the one to handle him.

My brother Burns takes twenty of them, and Jim takes eight
single pieces of property—including the one with the strange circle
chipped out of his teeth. "Can't wait to breed them," he says.
All his current slaves are up in years. "Now, that's smart business!"
I tell him. Good to keep these slaves mostly in the family, too.

It's a happy day when you can balance commerce and kinfolk.

"Foster," I say. "Why don't you take this bunch?
For all your hard work on the *Clotilda*." His eyes bug
out of his shocked, sickly little face. "You mean
I'm a slave owner now?" he says. I clap him on the back.
"You've earned it."

ABILẸ

WHAT'S WORSE THAN BEING WHIPPED

When Meaher pushes me, along with a few others,
     toward Captain Foster, I shake my head, reach
for Kêhounco. "My sister stays with me," I say.
     Kêhounco's eyes are wide

as she shrinks back. "No, no," she says. "They'll whip
     you again." I'm so startled to hear her voice
that I stop pulling. "You belong with me," I tell her.
     Tears fill her eyes as Meaher pushes

her toward the one they call Burns. I can't breathe
     as Foster leads me away from her. How can
they split all of us up like this? Me to Foster, Kêhounco
     to Burns, Kossola to the one they call Jim.

KÊHOUNCO
PARTING SONG

Nineteen others walk beside me, but without Abilè I may as well be alone.

Abilè, my sister, my friend. Already I miss her gentle hands,
her soft voice singing me through the days and nights.

I'm about to cry out when I hear her voice. "Kò ní séwu lọ́nà." A song for
travelers, a wish for no dangers on the road. I tuck my shell into my cheek and lift my
voice. Soon our song drowns out the mosquitoes as our family of survivors is divided.

GUMPA
NEVER-ENDING PARADE

After the sale of our bodies, we walk, clothes draping off our frames as we shuffle along in a ragged procession.

I keep my spine ramrod straight, head held high, suffering in silence, staying strong for the group.

Anytime the white men see people advancing in our direction, they drive us into the bushes to hide.

Mosquitoes continue to hum and feast while our own stomachs clench in hunger.

The sky is bright blue and endless.

KUPOLLEE
THE SOUND OF HOME

From
behind
bushes, we
see a parade
of costumed people
and animals. When a
trumpet cuts the air, my heart
lifts. An elephant! For a long
moment it even smells like we're home.

KOSSOLA

DE ELEPHANT'S PROMISE

I can't believe it when I see that
elephant coming down de road.
So bold and proud—de ground shakes
each time it takes a step. De air fills
with screams of delight. "Àjànàkú! Àjànàkú!
Ilé! Ilé!" That means "Elephant! Elephant!
Home! Home!" in Yorùbá and Fon.
I forget for a moment that I'm naked,
chained to seven others, following de white
man called Jim, in a land far, far from my home.
Forget that I'm walking away from Abilè,
Kupollee, and Gumpa. "Àjànàkú! Àjànàkú!
Ilé! Ilé!" Such a sight feels like a promise:
You will get back home. When de elephant's
call splits de air, it says to me: *Don't give up.*

TIMOTHY

ALL THE RIGHT MOVES

With the sale out of the way, it's time to take my thirty-two pieces of cargo to one last hideaway, three miles from my estate on Telegraph Road. It's called Grub Swamp. I'll keep them there until the US Marshal stops following me like a hound dog in his hopeless search for the slaves.

VII.

ENSLAVED
JULY 1860–APRIL 1861

MARY

WELCOME TO TELEGRAPH ROAD

When thirty-two new slaves walk up the drive,
a wife must pull on her boots.
For a plantation runs much like a hive:
When thirty-two new slaves walk up the drive,
show them their cabins, have Noah ward off disputes.
Don't gape at their skin or filth when they arrive.
When thirty-two new slaves walk up the drive,
a wife must pull on her boots.

KUPOLLEE

NEW LIFE

After the barracoon, *Clotilda*,
the swamp, we move to slave cabins
with roof, walls, floor. A table,
and beds stuffed with corn husks.
When the white wife hands
us shirts, pants, shoes,
we don't know
what to
do.

KOSSOLA

LEARNING A NEW WAY OF LIFE

Dey march my group across de fields
to Jim Meaher's plantation.
"Where are de cabins?" I ask when
we get to his small house. It isn't grand
like Telegraph Road at all. Dey order
us to crawl under de house, into de
tight space between de floorboards
and de brick-covered earth. We sleep
beside de dogs and chickens—
except when de heat and de mosquitoes
make sleep impossible. Between slapping,
itching, and dripping sweat while being
pressed up so close to one another,
it's almost like being back on board *Clotilda*.
When dawn comes, dey order us up
and out, and my eyes burn from lack
of sleep. It takes a minute for my arms
and legs to stretch and unfold. Dey march
us out to de fields, where we meet up
with de other shipmates. I can't help
smiling when I see Abilè and de others.
And we're all glad when dey start handing
out clothing, though it takes days for us to get
accustomed to de new garments. So stiff
and scratchy! A black man called Noah,
who has a bad leg, shows us how to
put our feet in de pants and work de latch.

He helps us with de strange shirtsleeves
and buttons. My feet sink into new shoes—
at least our feet are covered.

TIMOTHY
COURT DATE

I stroll into the courtroom pumping hands,
    whispering a word or two of meaningless
balderdash into the ears of a curious public.
    I have to stop myself from casting a knowing
wink at Judge Jones as I state—under oath—that
on July 7th, despite their claiming I sailed the *Clotilda* into
Mobile with a shipload of Negroes, I was actually serving
    supper and cards to guests on the *Roger B. Taney*.
When my claims are all confirmed by witnesses,
    I'm absolved of any allegations.

I don't stick around for any backslapping, though,
    because this business has already taken up
too much of my time. I press my horse to a
gallop all the way home to Telegraph Road.

KOSSOLA

MY NEW NAME

After a few days, dey line us up
to put our names in their books.
Jim Meaher asks, "What is your name?"
Thanks to Noah, and Kupollee on de ship,
I already know some English words.
I sing it out de way my ìyá always did.
Jim tries to make de shape of my name
in his mouth, but he adds a bumblebee
sound in de middle. "No," I say and break
it down for him. "Ko. Su. La." He throws
up his hands. "Doesn't matter. You'll
answer to whatever I decide to call
you." De reason my name's getting
put in Jim's book is because he bought
me. Still, I want to be sure I understand
correctly, that I'm enslaved. My words come
out breathy, weak. "Am I your property?"
A slow smile lifts his cheeks. "That's right.
I'm your master now." In that moment
I have nothing that's my own. Not one thing—
except my name. If he can't say my real name,
I want to choose for myself, one his mouth
can make. "Call me Cudjo." He repeats it
perfectly, so that's what goes in de book.
It's a strong name from Africa that means
"born on a Monday." Doesn't change who
I am on de inside. I will always be Kossola,
no matter what de white men call me.

WILLIAM
THE FAME GAME

Because I successfully steered
those slaves onto these Alabama
shores—and got away with it,
mind you—I now attract eyes on me
faster than a hummingbird finds nectar.

You'd think the sentence "Captain
Foster, so nice to meet you" is my actual
name, because I hear it on an endless
loop. Fame brings me handshakes,
pats on the back, and fake laughter.

I thought I'd like all this attention,
but I don't. Most days now I want
to be left alone. If there's any good
news lately, it's I've taken a bride.
Her name is Adelaide.

Plus, I'm now a slave owner. Captain Tim
was more excited about it than me.
We'll see how that goes. Downside is
all this success cost me my ship.
I miss the *Clotilda*.

ABILẸ

FIRST DAYS WITH FOSTER

New room, new clothes, new name. Foster writes
        in his book: "Celia." And from that moment on,
that's what he and Mrs. Foster call me. It takes a while for me
            to learn to answer to the strange-sounding syllables.

Everything is new and different. Through it all I watch for
        Kêhounco, hoping she'll appear. I don't understand how
we've gone from prisoner to slave. It feels like all I do is wait—
            which leaves far too much time for my heart to hurt.

KOSSOLA
WORKING DE FIELDS

Another week passes, maybe two.
When Timothy Meaher arrives,
I'm glad to see him—glad to finally
have something to do. De tenseness
in my back and neck eases just knowing
there's a purpose for us, a job to do.
If dey need us for something, it's less
likely dey will kill us.
But when Meaher shows us de fields
and demonstrates how to put de mule
behind de plow, my eyes about pop
out of my skull. Back home
we use a hoe for that kind of work.
Back home no one stands over us.
No one barks out orders. No one gets
whipped for going too slow. Back home
we are free. Here in America, everything's
different. What good is it to know how
deep to press in de yam seeds when dey
don't grow yams in Alabama? It's like
I'm a child, starting all over again.
And de Meaher brothers are sticklers
about time and how it must be used
to save—or make—money. Dey work
us every moment that's not pitch-black.
We labor long before de birds tweet
"good morning" and long after de coyotes
screech "good night."

KÊHOUNCO
LIFE WITHOUT ABILẸ̀

I wish Abilẹ̀ was here with me at Burns Meaher's estate, where they call me "Lottie."

We twenty shipmates are added to the nineteen slaves already here—I sing to help comfort the young ones, and the slave named James helps us learn their words.

They put me in the Big House, where I'm expected to help in the kitchen and tend the garden. Mostly I'm alone, except for Martha, the house slave in charge. I do the counting game and sing Abilẹ̀'s songs so that she is always with me.

JAMES

EMPATHY

The Africans shield
themselves from others. I think
our language and theirs
are too distant to shake hands.
My hope is that changes soon.

Some Negroes laugh at
how the Africans first wore
clothes with shirttails wrapped
around midsections, putting
legs through shirtsleeves. I like it.

Perhaps they did that
to mimic how each dressed in
their homeland? I feel
drawn to them. Yes, Kêhounco
has something to do with it.

When I go to sleep
each night, I can hear their cries
pierce the lilac skies
with loneliness and pain that
breaks the moon open.

ABILẸ̀

ONCE CAPTAIN, NOW MASTER

It's strange seeing Foster as a man who walks on land.
      All those weeks on *Clotilda*, I'd see his thin frame
and long beard and think he only existed in that world
          of water. But here he is, my master—

though he doesn't seem all that happy about it. "What
      good are these slaves anyway," Foster says over
coffee and blueberry muffins. "I could improve our situation
          faster if only we hadn't been forced to burn *Clotilda*."

Each day I learn new words. Each day I look for Kêhounco.
      When, after weeks, we pass one another while
she's in Burns's garden and I'm on my way to collect water,
          it's like I've swallowed the sun

and it's rising inside me. Yet I don't dare call out.
      I simply stare at her with all my energy, begging her
to see me. It takes only a second before her bright eyes
          lock onto mine, and an ocean of stories passes

between us. "My cheetah-sister," I whisper, glad to see she's
      dressed in fine garments, not a field hand's rags.
Though I've heard what it's like to work inside, always
          being watched and no free time.

I smile at Kêhounco, because that's all I can do—smile
      and hope she doesn't break a bowl or displease
the mistress. If only we could choose our work. But, no, they
          don't listen to us. Here we have no choices at all.

KOSSOLA

DECKHAND DAYS

Dey put me to work on a steamer.
Up and down de Alabama River we go,
delivering goods and passengers.
Nothing in my old life could have prepared
me for de rough and rowdy river life.
Meaher's steamers pack hard-faced white
men who stay liquored up
and are quick to lift their fists. I try to
be invisible and focus on my job handling
de cotton. De best days I'm assigned
de job of rollodore—de person rolling
de giant cotton bale across deck
and down de slideway to de stevedore,
who moves de bale onto de landing.
Gravity and fresh air sure do help ease
de load! Not like de agony of hooking cotton
bales to lift them on board, or hauling cords
of wood to feed de hot-flame engine.
Oh, de heat! Sweat rivers down my back
as we make deliveries at hundreds of stops
along that stretch of Alabama River
between Mobile and Montgomery. De heat
sits so heavy in my lungs that it weakens my legs.
If we accidentally drop a bale, or if we don't
move them fast enough, de overseer
yanks his whip from its holster. Then de heat
turns sharp and tastes like blood.
De heat feasts on our skin and singes

our souls. Our bodies shrivel
under de Alabama sun de way cornstalks do
when de rains forget to come.

TIMOTHY
SHOWTIME

Folks sure are curious about my slaves.
"Never seen them so black," they say. "From which distant
land did you snatch them?" I'm tempted to tell them
some wild story, but sometimes, especially today, I'm
bored with the whole thing, and tired. I take a deep breath,
then come up with some fresh balderdash to throw at them.

"Listen, everyone," I tell my passengers. "There's
no difference between slaves from America and Africa.
You couldn't tell them apart no more so than, let's say,
a family of ants. A slave is a slave is a slave."
To prove my point, I grab a boy named Bully.
"Where are you from?" I say. "South Carolina," he answers.
"How are you?" I say. He pats his belly.
"I'm blessed and so's my tummy."
One of the passengers then inquires about the filing
of his teeth and the scars on his face. "Smallpox,"
I say. "And those teeth make his meals go down easier.
Isn't that right, Bully?" He hunches his shoulders, then
starts to dance—just like I've told him to do. Distraction
is a wonderful tool to avoid potential problems.
As expected, everyone laughs, and my energy returns.
We should be a circus team, I tell you!

ABILĖ

SHOE STORY

At the end of our first cotton harvest, they let us gather
      in the evenings—all of us shipmates again in one place.
We light a fire to keep warm. Kupollee right away goes
          to sharing memories of home—

òrìṣà traditions and how delicious the fruit. Others join in,
      sharing family stories. "Your turn," Kossola says, and I glare
at him. "I've got no memories," I say. He knows I can't look back,
         will never look back. "I won't give up," he says,

his chipped teeth flashing. I nudge Kêhounco with my toe. "Tell
      them about your sisters," I urge. She shakes her head at me.
"You tell them." So I do. And while I'm telling it, I notice Kêhounco
        isn't wearing shoes. I stop the story.

"That Burns gives you fine skirts but no shoes?" Her lips make
      a thin line. "He says our feet will toughen without shoes."
I kick my boots off. "Take these." Her big eyes get even bigger.
        "I can't take yours. They're too big anyway."

I duck into a cabin, where I pull corn husks out of the mattress.
      "We'll stuff the toes with this." I help her ease her crusty feet
inside. "But now your feet will be cold," she says. I shrug, ready
        to return to the story. "I've been cold before."

KOSSOLA

DE DOG AND DE TORTOISE

That night I tell my shipmates de story
of de dog and de tortoise—just one of many
Yorùbá parables about Ajapa de trickster.
It goes like this: Ajapa de tortoise and de dog
were friends. One day dey went together
to de farmer's field to steal some yams.
Soon Ajapa's basket was overflowing with yams—
far more than he could eat. Far more than he
could carry! He sang out for help. "Dog, help me
carry these yams!" De dog begged Ajapa to stop
singing. "De farmer will hear you, and he will
catch us!" To keep Ajapa quiet, Dog had no choice
but to help Ajapa with de yams. While he was
busy rearranging de basket, Ajapa slipped
into de woods—just as de farmer arrived.
"Thief!" de farmer said, and snatched up de dog.
He took him back to de farm, where he was chained
to de house. Meanwhile, Ajapa was left with
all de yams he could eat. "It means," I tell them,
"we must not be greedy. Better to be content."
Sighs and affirmations warm de air, and I can't
remember a time since we arrived in America
when I've felt more content. I'm with my African
brothers and sisters—my only family in this place.
I've got shoes, and now my friend Kêhounco does, too.

JAMES

RING OF TRUST

I'm eating lunch with
the Africans. I smile at
being allowed in
their ring of trust. When they tell
me stories of once having

freedom, my heart turns
heavy as stones in water.
"I've been a slave all
my life," I say with a flash
of jealous rage. "I've never

tasted a sip of
independence." Kossola
puts his hand on my
shoulder, whispers, "We're sorry."
I nod, whisper back, "Thank you."

WILLIAM

BURDENS

The *Clotilda* didn't need shoes.
Didn't need clothes or food, either.
Yet these slaves need each of those things.
For example: this one girl, her African name
is Abilẹ or somesuch, but we call her Celia.

She's working my last nerve.
Celia "lost" her shoes. How is that possible?
I should whip her until that black flesh
peels away like spoiled banana skin.
It probably wouldn't do any good.

Plus, all I hear or read about now is this
impending civil war, and the question of slavery.
I didn't come to America for this nonsense.
I have so many burdens. The world presses
down on me with the force of a tidal wave.

KUPOLLEE

THE DEATH OF FREEDOM

Crops
grow slow
on this land.
Our women are
forced into the field.
Our clothing thins to thread.
We shiver against winter's
chill, reach for blankets that aren't there.
We cry: Once we were free, now we're slaves.

TIMOTHY
CHANGE IN THE AIR

A cold snap has hit Mobile on this December morning.
Mary is at the table scribbling out plans for our
annual New Year's party. She's determined to bring in
the year 1861 in style. Gives her something to focus on.

I'm devouring the morning paper, happy as a pig in slop
after reading about President Buchanan's State of the
Union address. The president claimed no slaves have
been brought to American shores in breach of the law.
I can't decide whether he's clueless or just covering for folks
like me. I guess it doesn't matter really. Important thing is
I'm in the clear.

All week long after the president's speech, people buzz
in my ears, asking my opinion on new laws being passed
and the probability of a new confederacy being created.
Like I have all the answers. I may be famous, but I'm
only one man. Shouldn't come as a surprise that it's
Foster who gets on my last nerve. "What do you want
to be remembered for?" he asks me when we're cruising
the river together. "Look, Foster. I don't want to be
remembered for anything. That means you're dead."
I shake my head. "I got way too much living to do to
worry about that."

GUMPA
REVENGE

We purge our souls through songs, pushing through the horrors we face every day.

Winter becomes spring.

We sing so we do not end our lives by our own hands.

The white men miss no opportunity to shout, insult, and whip us.

Indeed, it is a miracle that our dignity has not melted like a slab of ice on a summer day.

Yet here we are—alive.

Gratitude and pride quickly shift to rage when the overseer denies us water, then tears into one of our women for collapsing from dehydration.

He rips away her dress, exposing her chest.

I drop my hoe, and the rest of my African brothers follow.

When we reach the white overseer with the whip, half of us seize him and the other half pull the pulp of a woman away from him.

Next thing I know, the lash is in my hands, and it is splitting white flesh so violently his ancestors' ancestors probably sense it.

I am told other slaves have been drawn and quartered for such behavior.

But this man does the opposite; he retreats.

"Your punishment will come later," the overseer promises, fear lighting his eyes.

KUPOLLEE

SUNDAY DANCE

Life
is dance,
and dance is
life. When we dance,
we are free—no slave
master in control. Our
bodies once again our own.
Time—for a moment—unmeasured.
Our hearts back home, in sweet Africa.

GUMPA

RESPECTFULNESS

This gentleman, Free George, wants us to read his Bible and pray with him—and he does not like our dancing.

He comes to me first, and I appreciate this gesture.

"Please stop this gyrating," he says, with urgency. "Sunday is for God."

Respectfulness is the key to solving many problems in life.

When I indicate that he may address the group, he says, "I once was a slave like you—until I invited Jesus Christ into my life."

"Jesus Christ made you free?" I ask.

"Yes, he blessed my wife with an owner who allowed her to buy her freedom."

The room rumbles with questions.

"Jesus Christ provided for us, and then my wife bought my freedom."

"That's how you get free in this country?" Abilè says. "Through Jesus Christ?"

Free George assures us that it is true.

We confer, and I make the announcement.

"We agree to stop dancing on Sunday."

Free George lifts his hands. "Give God the glory, trust in Jesus Christ, and blessings will flow into your life. Amen."

While I do not think Jesus Christ is the answer, I am just one.

Each must choose his or her own way of living in this country.

TIMOTHY
NIGHTTIME THOUGHTS

In public I expand my chest like an accordion,
but tonight as I sag into bed—careful not to wake Mary—
my mind and body are weary.

As 1861 comes to a close, I can't help
but think what a year it's been.

In January, our great state of Alabama left the Union,
then laid down a verdict against opening up the slave trade
again. We're now part of the Confederacy, and Jefferson
Davis is our new president of the Confederate States.
This whole thing is turning into a bona fide war!

My thoughts cyclone. How am I supposed to run a business
during a war? My slaves could be sent off to fight, whether
I like it or not. The Confederate Army may need
them to build a fortress around Mobile. Makes me
hotter than Satan's sweat. All this chaos—and for what? Equality?
The idea of slaves being treated equal to whites scorches my backside.
No one with darker-colored skin has any right to be my peer. It's sinful.

This new president of the United States, Abraham Lincoln,
is one darkie-loving poltroon. He ought to be strung up for undoing
all the good work Buchanan did for our proud nation.
I stare at the ceiling for a good long while before gravity finally
works its way to my eyelids, shutting them like a curtain.

VIII.

WHEN WAR COMES TO TOWN
APRIL 1861–APRIL 1865

KÊHOUNCO

THE WAR

I am just finished with the dusting when Burns and his wife depart for Mobile.

"Where are they going in such a hurry?" I ask Martha. "Don't you know?" she says in a chirpy voice. "The war has started." She smiles. "The war that will free us."

My insides tense, remembering the men who kidnapped me on the beach. War was what got me here, in America. Martha slaps the towel at me. "We ain't the ones who got to fight it. We just got to survive it. Go on now, get back to work."

JAMES

SEALED OFF

We slaves are sealed off
from the outside world tighter
than jars of preserves.
Yet something is happening
around these parts, because we

hear gunshots popping
off in the distance. Feels like
we're being swallowed
up by fireworks—when will
it stop? Also, food's in short

supply. We used to
get fresh scraps from Master Burns—
now hardly any
of us get a blessed thing.
Our poor stomachs scream for food.

Today a white man
offered a bunch of carrots
to his chestnut horse
while we watched. "Mmm-mmm," he said,
then galloped away, laughing.

KUPOLLEE
A SLIVER OF HOPE

War?
Hard to
believe it.
We still labor
each day, we still get
whipped. Only now there's less
to eat—thanks to the Union
blockading Southern ports. "Maybe,"
I tell Kossola, "soon we'll be free."

KOSSOLA

WARTIME

Some things change during de war,
like how de Meahers have us plow under
their cotton fields and make us grow
other crops, like corn—because we can
eat corn. Most nights my stomach grumbles
for lack of sustenance, and we just about
never have any meat. De dock's full
of stories about starvation and desperation.
One woman in Tensaw gets sold for a sack
of salt! De Meahers don't sell any of us,
but dey do finally have us kill off a bunch
of de hogs. "Can't have those Africans
dying on me," Master Timothy says
to Noah. "Not after all the trouble I went
through to get them." When I tell Abilẹ
about it, my mouth waters in anticipation
of pig ears and bacon. "See?" I say. "Dey
don't want to eat us, Abilẹ. Dey want to feed
us." She rolls her eyes at me. "We're too
skinny to eat," she says. "Our bones aren't
good for anything but soup." We lean into
one another. "You're different than you used
to be," I tell her. "You're not scared anymore."
She shakes her head. "I'm still scared.
I'm just better at hiding it."

TIMOTHY
PORCH TALK

Burns and I relax on his porch, packing a smidgen less
tobacco into our pipes—on account of the Southern
barricade now blocking goods from being delivered
to the fine citizens of Alabama.
We do our part by eating and drinking two-thirds
of what we normally do. "This is nice," I tell Burns.
It's a pleasure to visit my brother's land once in a while.
"I need more slaves," Burns says. "Well," I say,
"stop whining and do something about it.
That James of yours, now, he's a stud if I ever did see one.
Time for him to marry, spread his seed, and get one
of those women pregnant."
Burns nods his head. "You're right."
I whack him on his shoulder. "Of course I am.
You should always listen to your big brother."

JAMES
MARRIAGE

No one's more shocked than
me when Master Burns says, "You're
getting married and
starting a family with
Kêhounco." I'm so thankful!

It's coming up on
a year since I first saw her,
filthier than dirt,
hacking in sickness—convinced
she was an African queen.

I heard Africans
are cannibals who also
stomp around, sever
heads off innocent people.
I never believed all that.

Doesn't bother me
that she keeps a tiny shell
tucked under her tongue,
either. What it means is she's
trustworthy, loving, and true.

KÊHOUNCO

WEDDING DAY: JUNE 12, 1861

When they told me I must marry James, I wanted to be Abilè's cheetah and run.

But I didn't run. All it would get me was a beating. I knew I had no choice—though I should be home with my sisters, giggling over my parents' match for me.

Not forced to marry an American slave so that we will produce more slaves. I know that's what they want. Like we're hogs in a pen. At least James is kind. He fed us, and he didn't turn away from me during those mosquito-days in the canebrake.

ABILẸ
ABOUT MARRIAGE

In the days following the wedding, Kêhounco is always
        on my mind. She's strong, I tell myself. She'll be fine.
When I finally see her, relief crawls out of my throat as a squeal.
        She grabs my hands and speaks quickly.

"He treats me well. We're learning each other's words
        and ways. We get along." I smile. "My cheetah-sister,
a wife!" She smiles back. "You'll be next," she says.
        "I hope they pick Kossola for you."

I shake my head, though I hope so, too. Kossola is gentle
        when other men are not. But how can I think of a husband
when my parents— No, I will not go there. Not now, not after all this time.
        I focus on Kêhounco. "I'm so happy for you, sister."

GUMPA
PRIDE OF THE FON

A year passes, then another.

Ever since that time when together we swarmed the overseer, our owners keep a healthy distance from us, especially when we are all assembled.

The punishment that was promised comes in the form of extra work that keeps us slaving into the dark hours.

As a young boy my dreams did not include meeting my future wife on a slave ship, being married, and starting a family on this foreign land that was not part of my heritage, where a sickly dog is cared for better than me.

Yet like sweet blankets of rain coming down while the sun shines, life is full of surprises.

I first saw Josephine in the barracoon back in Africa.

After arriving on this strange land, we had time to bond over being snatched from our world of glory and cast into this world of suffering.

Despite being on foreign soil, our hearts lighten in matrimony and soar even higher with the birth of our son, Leroy.

We tattoo on his chest an image of Dan Ayidohwèdo—the rainbow snake biting its own tail.

This is the holy emblem for my religion, the Fon.

May all who meet Leroy know he is blessed, that he comes from a proud people.

These white men can try to erase our existence with their own customs, but they will never stop our love of our African homeland—or of each other.

MARY

A DEFINITION OF WAR

War means doing without:
No sweets for little Augustine, and Timothy's always gone.
"Coffee" made from burnt rice is much too stout!
War means doing without—
who's ever heard of a sugar drought?
For Augustine, I tell myself: "Just hang on."
War means doing without:
No sweets for me. My faith in Timothy's almost gone.

TIMOTHY
BLOCKADE RUNNER

These days, roughly two years into the war, I spend more time
on my ships as a blockade runner. We ship cotton to Cuba
in exchange for casks of fabric, alcohol, foodstuff,
weapons, and ammo. I make these death-defying trips to do my part
for the Confederacy, and also to fill my pockets with money.
It's dangerous work, and I miss my Mary and Augustine so much
that if I think about it too often, my heart won't be able to handle it.
Instead, I focus on the wheel and the water, thankful I'm not required
to serve as a soldier. God bless the new law passed by the Confederate
Congress! It guarantees that any white man who owns a plantation
with twenty or more slaves is exempt from military service.
Whoever created this law deserves a free pour
of expensive Southern whiskey for being a tried-and-true,
red-white-and-blue American. And for those who don't qualify
for the exemption? Well, it's not my fault there are poor
whites out there who don't know how to run a successful business.
That's their road to travel, not mine.

GUMPA
NOTICING

Most of the time, these white people go about their business like we are invisible.

They do not notice us noticing bushy-bearded men dressed in gray uniforms knocking on Master Timothy's door, asking for "darkies on your property."

They want us to build barricades to help defend the Confederate territories.

They also do not notice us noticing how this does not make Master Timothy happy at all.

How he now walks around, pacing back and forth with furrowed brow, muttering to himself, looking as if the world is sitting on his shoulders.

And we know why: The more of us they take to use for the war, the less of us there are here to work—which means less profit for Master Timothy, and more work for the ones left behind.

To white people, we are a combination of machine and beast.

To us, white people are nothing more than cowards and demons.

KOSSOLA

SWEET EVENINGS

Even during de war we Africans
gather whenever we can. "Look at that
starswept sky," Gumpa says one evening
after our meal. "A reminder of home."
We all agree, and Gumpa shares with us
something he overheard. That's how we get
most of our information—by listening.
"Yesterday," Gumpa says, "Master Timothy
and his brothers spoke of a runaway slave
by the name of Andrew. They caught him
in the woods, and now he is locked up,
awaiting his penalty." I drop my head,
because I don't believe this story can have
a happy ending. For a long moment, de only
sound in de room is de chickens clucking
from their roosts beneath de floorboards.
"I envy the ones who get off this plantation
to go fight in the war," Gumpa says, finally.
"As for Andrew, at least he is brave and proud
enough to seek a life away from here.
Someday I would like to be so brave."
Several others nod their heads, but it's important
to me to be grateful. "Things could be worse
for us," I say. "At least here we know what
to expect on de property. Out there, who knows
how dey will treat us? Poor Andrew, his
punishment will be more painful than if
he didn't try to escape." Gumpa shakes

his head. "I am not sure about that, my friend."
I don't want to argue with him, so I go
back to de one thing I know we can all
agree on. "Once this war is over, and we're free,
I'm taking Abilẹ back home to Africa—
where no one needs sugar, because
de fruit trees always give fruit,
and life is naturally sweet."

TIMOTHY
MISFORTUNE

Once in a while I run into a little misfortune—
a man can't endure three years of war without it.

Just as I long feared, the Confederates take some
of my slaves to build barriers in order to
protect the city of Mobile.

Then on December 31, 1863, the Union Navy gives me
all sorts of fits when the USS *Kennebec*, led by that
poltroon W. P. McCann, seizes my ship the *Gray Jacket*
as we head to Cuba for another blockade run.

That's two failed blockade trips. My plan
to split with the Confederacy the earnings off the cotton
on board has disappeared. To make matters worse,
now they'll auction off my ship. All this is a definite
black eye for the Southern swashbuckler.
However, I still have another eye that hasn't been
touched yet. I see good things ahead for me.

JAMES

TAKING THE LEAP

From the time I was
a tender-footed, confused
child, I've been working
for Master Burns. Now I hear
freedom's siren! In August

1864,
the Union captures both Fort
Gaines and Fort Morgan,
so if anyone reaches
those camps without being caught,

freedom is theirs. I
share this news with Aunt Amy,
Kêhounco, and my
friend Luke. We all decide this
is finally our chance to

take a leap. The risk
is worth it. The glory of
emancipation
could be ours. The Meahers love
to bet; well, now, so do we.

KÊHOUNCO
ESCAPE

We leave on a Saturday night: me, James, and Aunt Amy.

We wait as long as we can for Luke, but he doesn't show up.
Neither does Abilę. She warned me it was too risky. But James is certain.

Frogs sing as we glide down the moonlit river toward Fort Morgan. I scan
the shore for lamplight. As I stroke the shell in my pocket, I listen for dogs.
The farther we get from Abilę, the harder my chest squeezes.

TIMOTHY
NO REST FOR THE WEARY

Can't a man have a moment's peace with his family?
I'm sitting in my rocking chair rereading *The Red Rover*
by James Fenimore Cooper next to Mary and Augustine
when Burns gallops up so out of breath he barely sputters
out the words: "Three of my slaves are missing. One of
them is James. Luke just told me. I've put together
a gang to find them." I slam my book on the table so
hard, Mary and Augustine's heads jerk. I swear
you can't trust darkies, no matter how good they act
in front of you. "Let's go!" I say, heading to my horse.

AUGUSTINE

RUNAWAYS

Right away my heart thump-thumps to think of Daddy
unleashing the dogs to hunt down the runaway slaves.
"Now, go on upstairs," Daddy says. My feet move slow
as sorghum syrup because I wish I knew a way to
warn the slaves—those dogs scare me with their
awful barks and pointy teeth. They run fast fast fast!
"You sick, son?" Daddy asks. I nod, glad three-year-olds must
stay at home, so I don't have to see those mean dogs.

TIMOTHY
BETRAYAL

With the help of our dogs following the scent of the slaves,
me and Burns dash all the way to where the Mobile River
splits in two directions before we abandon our pursuit
because there's no clear path for the horses.
They neigh in frustration as we pull their reins.
The dogs circle round and round, barking at the sky.
They've lost the scent. "These hounds are worthless!" I say.
Burns spits tobacco on the ground. "There's another
gang that's headed south. Maybe they'll have better luck."
His face creases in pain at their betrayal. "For more than
three years now, I've treated them so well."
I pat his shoulder. "I know, Burns, I know."

JAMES

ON THE RUN

I hold the hands of
Kêhounco and Aunt Amy.
My guts thrash and crash
as our boat drifts downriver.
When we hear clicking sounds, I

scan the shore, spy a
row of white men with rifles
aimed at us. My heart
clenches as our sweet dreams of
liberty melt away like

morning fog. Is this
how it all ends? Before I
have a chance to taste
freedom? To be somebody?
To prove that my life matters?

We're now a bullet
away from death. I slowly
breathe to keep myself
from shaking like tree branches
during a June thunderstorm.

We each clasp our hands
tighter. "No matter what," Aunt
Amy says, "they can't
beat our spirits. They can hurt
our bodies, not our souls." When

they step on the boat,
I sing out the first verse of
"Bound for the Land of
Canaan," until I'm met with
a rifle against my skull.

ABILÈ

PUNISHMENT

I wake to Foster's voice. "Captain Timothy said we should
     show them what we do to runaways." Mrs. Foster's
reply is small, desperate. "But it's wash day." Foster
     sighs. "It won't take long."

He loads all of us into the wagon and drives us to
     Telegraph Road. Over every bump and rut,
I worry and speculate about who the runaways are—
     Gumpa? Kossola? James? Oluale? I never

thought it would be Kêhounco until I see her standing
     with James and Amy in the center of the circle of slaves.
A cry burbles out of my throat. I told her not to do it!
     Kossola wraps his arms around my waist

to stop me from barreling toward her. "You can't go over there,"
     he says. "Or else dey will whip you, too." I know he's right,
I know he is. I sink into him. "Oh, my cheetah-sister."
     Kêhounco doesn't cry out as the whip slices

her skin again and again. Kossola covers my mouth
     so I won't cry out, either. "Go back home," he whispers.
"Home to Africa." For the first time since I was captured,
     I let myself back into my village, back through

the yard outside our adobe house, past the garden,
     past the fire, and inside the door. Where I am
a child surrounded by love—before everything went
     so horribly wrong. When I was still innocent.

KUPOLLEE
CLARITY

Another year passes, and the noose
of war tightens. "It cannot last,"
Gumpa says. Nearly five years
in this country, and we
aren't free yet. As spring
blows in warm skies,
we press seeds
into
soil.

TIMOTHY

WAR REPORT

The month of April 1865 is an avalanche of bad news.
No sooner do I pry open my eyes after another fitful night's
sleep than I'm knocked sideways by repeated death knells.
How has it come to this?

April 1: Our poor Confederate men are no match
for when the Union starts their onslaught of Mobile.

April 8: As Spanish Fort falls, an additional incursion bedevils
Fort Blakeley. The whole county—bay and bayou—is aflame.

April 9: In Appomattox County, Virginia, one of the greatest
Americans who's ever drawn breath, Robert E. Lee, surrenders.

April 10: Early-morning chimes clang against the steely
skies, calling our fine men in uniform to withdraw
from Mobile. I see soldiers divesting
themselves of their weapons, tossing their bullets
into the river, dismantling and burning their rifles
before heading back home.

My throat threatens to regurgitate my morning eggs.
I don't recognize this new America.
How can the Confederacy be lost?

KOSSOLA

ONE UNFORGETTABLE DAY: APRIL 12, 1865

De fog hangs spooky over de river
de way it does sometimes in spring,
and we know it might be a while before
Captain Tim arrives on de *Southern
Republic*. He won't like us getting behind
schedule, so we all stand around easy-like
on that Montgomery dock, enjoying de time
while we've got it. Before long, de sun
burns away de fog, and de river's clear
as anything, de banks thickening with green
and azalea blossoms. "Sure is quiet," I say.
No river traffic to speak of. Not far past
us a Union soldier's loafing off, plucking
mulberries from a tree and popping them
into his mouth. "What's going on?" Noah asks.
De soldier moseys over. "Haven't you heard?
War's over." My whole body goes rigid.
Did he really say what I think he said?
Noah finds his voice before I do. "You mean
we're free?" he says. "We can leave?"
De soldier shrugs. "I reckon so." I jump
up like I've been electrified, and we all
start dancing around de dock. "Free" is de word
we've all been dreaming of. "Where
are we supposed to go?" Noah says.
"Wherever you want," de soldier replies.
We hurry away without another thought
for Captain Tim or de river or de cargo

waiting to be loaded. It's not our problem
anymore. We bundle our shoes and hats
and stride right off that dock. "Thank you,"
I say to each person we pass—white, black,
soldier, deckhand, everyone. Mo dúpẹ́,
mo dúpẹ́, mo dúpẹ́. We're FREE!

TIMOTHY
LOST AT SEA

I should be at home protecting my family,
shielding them in case these freed darkies—no doubt
ginned up on alcohol—start running wild, storming
our thoroughfares, ransacking windows
with slabs of stone and bricks. Instead, I'm on board
my favorite ship, the *Southern Republic*, commissioned
by the government to reclaim ammunition and other supplies
that once belonged to the Confederacy.
Sure as the sun climbs out of the ocean
each morning, the South will rise again.

KÊHOUNCO

THE END

No one tells me the news, but I overhear it from the kitchen during lunch.

"War's over," Burns says. The pot Martha's washing clatters into the sink, and our eyes meet. "We free now?" Martha says.

My whole body goes still with listening to Burns explain it to his wife.
I'm not even sure I know anymore what the word "free" means.
But if what they're saying is true, then no one is going to stop me from finding out.

ABILÈ
WASTED TIME

When I hear the news, my mind lightnings
    to Kêhounco, to the stripes on her back, scars
from the time when she and James tried to run away.
        If we're free, then I'm not wasting

another minute. I walk into the Fosters' parlor,
    my feet propelled by some deep force.
Mr. Foster slumps in his chair, his fingers stroking
        his scraggly beard. "You heard right—

you're free." Beside him, Mrs. Foster's face crumples.
    "Please don't go," she says to me. But I don't
listen. My feet are moving cheetah-fast. Kêhounco, I think.
        Kossola, Gumpa, Kupollee. We're free!

KÊHOUNCO

AN ANSWER TO THE QUESTION OF FREEDOM

It doesn't take more than a minute for me and James to gather our things.

My heart pounds with excitement, and with fear: Is it true?
Are we really free? As we walk away, I turn to look behind me.

No one follows us. No dogs howl. I place my hand in my pocket, finger
the shell—my one treasure from Africa. My legs tremble, and my feet
wobble in Abilẹ's too-big-for-me boots. "Abilẹ," I say. "We'll go to Abilẹ."

KUPOLLEE

MIRACLE

We
shipmates
gather in
the road. We cry.
We hug. "We can go
back home now," Kossola
says. "Five years they stole from us,"
Gumpa says. "We are together,"
I say. "Our family's free at last!"

GUMPA
FREEDOM DRUM

After years of walking like a herd of cattle with heads weighed down, muscles screaming, and feet dragging across the dirt, now our bones are lightened by freedom.

My African brothers and I venture into the forest, our backs straighter than fence posts.

I take my ax to a hollow tree stump, cut it free with a series of slashes, and shape it into a drum.

Together we kindle a fire and dance with our African sisters.

"Freedom!" we shout. "Òmìnira! Òmìnira! Òmìnira!"

IX.

THE TRUTH ABOUT FREEDOM
APRIL 1865–DECEMBER 1869

ABILẸ
REALITY

After the fire and the drum, dawn shows us
      old problems. "I don't think these shoes
will make it all the way back to Africa," I say.
           Kêhounco lifts her foot. "Mine, either."

"Then we'll get you new shoes," says Kossola.
      He is all smiles and good spirits. "How?"
asks Kêhounco. Her eyes shine out of her face,
           wider and brighter than ever.

Her skin practically glows in the early-morning
      light, and when she moves, it is not with
the cheetah-quickness I've come to expect.
           My brow creases as I watch her.

When James grabs her hand and squeezes,
      I know. I pull her to the side, whisper in her
ear. "You're pregnant?" Her cheeks lift, and
           she nods. "A little."

I clasp her to me, both of us laughing. You can't
      be "a little" pregnant. But I know what she
means. She's not far along, which is why no one
           else knows yet. It reminds me of—

I shake away the thought. "Home is a long way
      from here," I say. "We need to decide what
to do right now, today. Where will we live? How
           will we feed ourselves?"

The group falls silent for a moment. "Abilè's right," Gumpa says. "We need a plan."

Kossola hoists the drum on his shoulder. "We'll figure it out one step at a time."

KOSSOLA

HEADING SOUTH

Our first full day of freedom! How bright
de sunshine, how joyful my heart. Africa
suddenly so close I can taste it. Oh,
to be back in Bantè! Five years since we
came to this country on de *Clotilda*.
We didn't know anything then. But now
we know how to work de American crops,
ride de river, and speak de language.
"Let's go to Mobile," I say. "Get everyone
together who came across. We'll find work,
save up. Then we'll find a ship to carry us
home." I know it's a good idea when Abilẹ
smiles at me. "I think my shoes can make it
to Mobile," she says. It makes me happy
to see her happy. We join de mass
of dark-skinned bodies walking away
from slavery and toward new lives.
Whether pushing carts or hauling baskets
on their heads, everyone surges forward
with excitement—except for James.

JAMES
CALL OF FREEDOM

I wish I felt pure
joy like the others, but I'm
conflicted—I want
to go, but I keep thinking:
I should be in uniform.

All of my life, I've
never earned money for the
work I've done, or felt
a sense of belonging to
something greater than myself.

Now here's my big chance!
Even though the war may be
over, who's to say
it'll stay that way? I may lack
knowledge, but I'm not stupid.

Even though we're "free,"
I know the white man can snatch
away your freedom
faster than a rattlesnake
can strike. I promise you that.

As we're heading out,
my feet stop in the dirt road.
Kêhounco reaches
for my hand. "It's okay, James,"
she says. "You're one of us now."

Tears roll down my face.
"Please forgive me, Kêhounco.
I can't go. I need
to use my freedom to make
sure our country remains free.

"It's about duty—
you must serve your country, and
I must serve mine, too."
She shakes her head. "Kêhounco,"
I say, "I need to enlist."

KÊHOUNCO

PROMISE TO MY UNBORN CHILD

"Don't do this," I say to James. "I'm carrying your child."

His face momentarily brightens, and then he pushes his shoulders back. "All the more reason for me to enlist," he says. "So I can provide for our family."

My gaze follows Abilè. "Please, James." He drops his head. "You go." My steps are heavy as I walk away from him, but I don't look back. Placing my palm across my still-flat belly, I make a promise to our child: "I'll give you a family. *My* family."

JAMES

HEADING NORTH

I sign up for three
years in the Union Army
on April 19th,
1865. Even
though I miss Kêhounco and

our unborn baby,
I know I've made the right choice.
With the war over
they need men to help preserve
law and order. I travel

the streets on foot in
my uniform, a gun and
sword by my side. A
surge of hope and dignity
fills my soul as I march to

join my troop. I see
burned buildings sporting bullet
holes. People fill the
streets, their eyes hollow, dragging
their shuffling, weak, skeletal

bodies around with
nowhere to go. I accept
my mission to help
keep the peace, though I flinch when
the army cuts off my braids.

ABILẸ
WALKING TO MOBILE

No one is happier than me when
      Kêhounco shows up. "James enlisted,"
she says, her lips pressed together tight. "I'm going
          with you." I hug her to me.

"It will be okay," I say. But as we enter
      the road, we find it thick with former slaves—
all of them dragging their belongings and unsure
         of their destinations, just like us.

When a man and his wife join us for a while, they share
      a story. "Master at the next plantation over was so
desperate to keep his field slaves that he refused to let
         them go free," the man tells us.

"He shot them instead." I grab Kossola's arm to steady
      myself. The wife leans in. "On up near Selma, a master
cut off his slaves' ears." My steps get faster as they talk,
         because I want to get there—to freedom—

as soon as we can. "Slow down," Kêhounco says.
      "You can't outrun this." I know she's right, but my feet
still quicken as we pass a family resting on a tattered quilt in a ditch.
         I push my shoulders back. I will not die—not now.

TIMOTHY

SAD STATE OF AFFAIRS

These darkies that I fed and gave a day off once a week,
who used to speak with joy in their voices at being
on my property, now stare at me with eyes
hardened like stone. They've lost all their manners
and bark back to me with more sass than I did to
my own father when he poked fun at me for first
putting on a sailor's cap.

I don't see how they're ever going to be successful.
Each of them are too stupid to handle their own business.
Gracious, they're liable to starve to death with their new freedom.
They don't know nothing about nothing, and now we're turning
them loose? They need us as much as we need them.

Plus, I don't know how I'm going to keep my shipping
empire going without their free labor. I mean,
how am I supposed to run things with no slaves?
For the first time in many a year, I have doubts
about the future. What kind of world will I leave
behind for Augustine?

KUPOLLEE
A TASTE OF FREEDOM

What
a strange
thrill: to walk
without a pass!
No white men checking
our papers or telling
us what to do. Freedom tastes
different now—sunshine, yes, but
we must be careful not to get burned.

KOSSOLA

DAUPHIN STREET

Takes us all day to walk de few miles
to Mobile. De roads are crammed with people
just like us—a slow river of black folk
and their belongings getting hung up
at every bend. When we arrive at Dauphin
Street, it's like freedom is more than a word:
It's a place, right here, right now.
Throngs of former slaves fill every alley
clear to de docks—like people come
to watch a parade, except there's no order
to it at all—and we *are* de parade.
My orò training comes back to me.
A sense of danger lifts de hair on my neck.
"We can't stay here," I tell de group.
De spirits of de elders fill my ears,
telling me Mobile will not be kind to us,
not like this. We may have escaped
Captain Tim and others like him,
and we may be surrounded by people
newly freed just like us—but that doesn't
make us safe. "We got to go back.
There's no place for us here. Even if
we can find lodging, who will hire us?
Everyone here will be seeking jobs, too."
De group discusses it, then Gumpa's
familiar voice finds my ears. "Kossola
is right," he says. "Let us rest, then we
must return to the Meahers—people

we know, and people who know us
and what we're capable of. Now they
will have to pay us to do their work."
As much as it troubles me to go back
to de Meahers, I am convinced it's for
de best. I am not sorry to pivot,
to leave de uncertainty and confusion
of Dauphin Street behind.

TIMOTHY
DEAL-MAKING

When a group of my former slaves arrives in my yard,
I hold back a grin. They want to work, and Lord knows I need them.
"Got a taste of the real world, did you?" I laugh.
"Not near as sweet as Telegraph Road, is it?"
Cudjo's face doesn't crack even a smile. He is all business.
"We're willing to work for a fair wage." It surprises me that none
of them want the jobs they knew as slaves—Cudjo wants to build
bricks and shingles, Kupollee is interested in stacking lumber,
others fancy railroad or lumber mill jobs. Fine by me.
"It's a deal," I say.

I offer them their old slave quarters to live in.
"But now you're going to have to pay rent." They agree.
As they head to their old cabins, I smile and shake my head.
My African colony is back again, only this time, they must pay
to live here. I do the calculations in my head. For their wages,
I'll give them a dollar a day for their sunup to sundown services.
And somehow, I'll get at least one extra, unpaid hour a day
out of them, you just watch. My brothers are going to be thrilled
with this arrangement.

These people are going to be "free" in name only.

KUPOLLEE

ONE DOLLAR A DAY

When
they pay
me, I am
filled with shame. Back
home, a free man works
only for himself—not
for others. Who am I now?
Not "slave," but still slaving. I want
more. This is not the life I desire.

JAMES
READ AND WRITE

Freedom to me means
having choices. I need to
take advantage of
this new independence to
get educated at last.

I ask my troop if
they share this feeling, too. I
get yeses from most
of them, so we tell Chaplain
Fred. He says even though there's

no school for us to
learn, there are teachers up north
who could help. He makes
it clear the monthly fee for
instruction will be fifty

cents to a dollar
per person. We split our pay
so each of us will
get lessons. Our group will learn
to read and write together.

ABILẸ
THE WAY THINGS CHANGE AND DON'T CHANGE

As the spring turns into summer, our lives
        are rooted by the gardens we plant
and tend. Everything else is a mess of new laws
        and the Meahers' desperation

for workers. Most days I forget I'm not still a slave.
        At least we live in community with one another,
in the old slave cabins. I live for the evenings, when we all
        gather together.

"You going to change your name?" Kêhounco says.
        "Doesn't matter what they call me," I say.
"For five years now I've answered to 'Celia,' and it's a fine
        word. But it's not who I am.

"I'll always be Abilẹ." Kêhounco nods. "I don't
        mind 'Lottie.' Too much trouble to change it now."
She pushes her shoulders back, decision made,
        then cradles her belly, which

has just barely begun to round. "Any news of James?"
        I ask. She shakes her head. "Nothing."
I grab her hand. "We need to learn to read and write.
        So you can send him a letter."

Kêhounco gives a tiny smile. "That'll only work
        if James learns to read and write, too."
I grin. "Well, nothing we can do about that.
        But we can get to learning, can't we?

"And then when the baby comes, we'll teach her."

As Kêhounco leans into me, I feel Kossola's eyes upon me. "What?" I ask him.

"Abilè," he says. "You sound like me!"

GUMPA
NAME CHANGE

Much as I do not relish living in a place I do not belong, I decide to wedge myself into this foreign region after our people gain "independence"—and I use that word with great caution.

In order to survive and draw less attention to my differences, I will cleave my identity like an apple.

When the white men and their government ask me my name, I decide on "Peter" as a first and "Lee" as the last.

Both are simple, unflashy names that do not hold any real meaning for me.

I will not give them any part of my full African name.

They do not deserve it.

I am impressed, though, when Ausy conjures up a name that gets listed as "Ossa Keeby," to honor the Kebbi River where he and his people fished in Africa.

What is most important when it comes to this name-change business is that to the Africans whom I love and live with, I will always be Gumpa the Fon.

KOSSOLA
ON BECOMING A LEWIS

First thing de government wants to do
in those confusing days just after de war
is count everyone. Each time I tell my name
to a census-taker, dey write it their own way:
Cudjoe, Cugo, Cujo, Kudjoe, Cager.
I don't care how dey spell it. What's important
to me is keeping something from Bantè,
something to always remind me—and them—
of my home in Africa. America may be
where I live, but it's not *home*. I don't
understand at first about taking a last name,
what dey call a surname. "Don't have
one," I tell de white man. He frowns at me,
then tries again. "What is your father's name?"
I tell him, "Oluale." De census-taker scratches
onto de piece of paper. "Okay, then.
Your surname is 'Lewis.'" He takes de "lu"
sound, that's all. I don't complain. Free or not,
it's never a good idea to argue with a white man.

KUPOLLEE
WHAT KOSSOLA WANTS

When Kossola comes to me after
ten hours of work, his face shining,
fingers twisting his hat, I
sit with him. "I want to
marry Abilè,"
he says. "She's home
to me." I
grin. "Do
it!"

While I am not ready to marry,
it delights me that they have found
love in this country. I have
never felt more hopeful.
"If children come, they
will carry sweet
Africa
in their
bones."

KOSSOLA
PROPOSING TO ABILẸ

It's strange to think about marrying
when my initiation into orò can never
be completed. Kupollee's de one to
advise me. He fingers de gold hoops
that came all de way from Africa.
"The elders would want you to have
a family," he says. I know he's
right, but that's not all that troubles me.
"I don't even know how to arrange it,"
I say. In Bantè, my parents would've
given Abilẹ's parents gifts. Dey would know
what I have to offer her without me
even saying it. And then our parents
would decide, yes or no. "This isn't
Bantè," Kupollee says. "This is America."
So I do what Americans do: On a blue-sky
afternoon, I get down on one knee. "Abilẹ,"
I say. "Will you be my wife?" Her eyes
don't widen with surprise. She doesn't
smile or hug me. She pulls me up to
standing, her hands warm in mine.
"First I must tell you my story. My secret.
From before the *Clotilda*." De air around
us turns heavy, thick. "You don't have to,"
I tell her. She puts her fingers to my lips
to shush me. "You've always said someday
I will tell you. Well, today is that day."

ABILẸ
CONFESSION

I don't stop talking until Kossola knows
      everything. "My uncle, he was a bad man.
He followed me back to our house on market
         day. He ripped my clothes, shoved me

to the floor." My voice trembles at first, so I draw
      the words up from the well of my belly.
"He laid on top of me." I force myself to meet Kossola's
         eyes. "He did what bad men do."

Tears spring into Kossola's eyes, and he lifts
      his hand to smooth my cheek, but I push
his fingers away. I must tell him the rest. "He left
         me in a ball on the floor. And that's when

I ran after him. I grabbed the still-hot fire poker.
      Kossola, I stabbed him in the back." Kossola doesn't
look away. "I brought such shame to my family. I killed
         my uncle for what he did to me."

The words hang in the air between us, but not
      like fog. Like I am a lioness calling my pride
to the feast. "And when Glèlè's soldiers raided our village,
         I let them take me,

to make it easier for my family." Images of my parents
      float to the surface, and this time
I let them. I face Kossola. I am stained,
         and I am a coward, but I am still here.

"You know all my secrets now." We wipe each other's tears.
        "You still want me?" I ask. He takes my hand.
"I've wanted to marry you since the *Clotilda*."
              My cheeks lift. "You'll take care of me?"

Kossola nods. "Got my job at de shingle factory.
        Been saving as much money as I can."
His bright face turns serious. "I won't hurt you,
        Abilè. I only want to love you."

With those words all the places inside me that
        once were frozen or empty now thaw and fill.
My heart floods like my home valley after the first
        rain of the season. "Yes," I shout. "Yes!"

KÊHOUNCO
GOOD NEWS

When Abilè comes to visit, we rock side by side on the front porch.

I play-push her, like we are girls. "You said 'yes'?" Abilè slaps at me. "You knew?" I link arms with her, tell her Kossola came to me. "And I can see it on your face."

Abilè puts her head on my shoulder. "My cheetah-sister," she says, stroking my melon-belly. "Baby's growing." I place my hand on top of hers, leave it there. "We must get home to Africa," Abilè says. "For our children."

KOSSOLA

DREAM REVIVED

We never set a wedding date.
Abilè and me, we just move in
together instead. We don't need de
US government to tell us we're
married. We don't need a piece of paper.
All we need is to sleep and wake up
and work together. "It's time for us
to go back," Abilè says one night
when we're snug beneath de sheets.
"Now that we're free." My breath catches
at de thought. "You think we can do that?"
I say. "How?" Abilè cups my face in her
palms. "There's nothing we can't do,
so long as we do it together." She's not
just talking about de two of us—she
wants this for all who came over on
de *Clotilda*. I press my lips to hers.
"We need to have a meeting. With all
de shipmates. Figure out a plan."

GUMPA
EMERGENCY MEETING

In the four years of war, and the months since we got our freedom from slavery, our families have come to include a number of children.

Their presence makes us think more and more about returning to Africa.

Which is why my small cabin is stuffed with my fellow Africans, including Abilè, Kossola, Kêhounco, Oluale, and Kupollee.

It is hotter than a kiln in here, yet we keep the windows closed so no one suspects anything.

The discussion during our emergency meeting?

Going home.

"I have seen it done before," I say.

"Twice, in fact.

"Prince Fruku came home to Dahomey from Brazil after almost twenty-four years.

"When I was a boy, my parents told me about a time in the 1830s when a legion of our people who had been deported—including our neighbors—came back from Cuba and Brazil."

Hope thickens the air in the room like dust during ọyé.

KUPOLLEE

URGENT

Talk
of home
twists my heart.
It seems so long
ago, and yet my
mind is a hoe, turning
the soil of memory. "We
must go *now*," I tell them. "Before
the spirit of death calls us. Now. *Now!*"

ABILẸ

THE SPIRIT OF FREEDOM

Kupollee's words arouse something in me—
      the longing in his face reminds me of all
my hopes for this life: children, family, belonging.
          Things Kossola and I have together,

but not outside of this circle of shipmates.
      "We can't stay here," I tell them. "This 'freedom'
means nothing. It's just a stupid word." Heat rises
         in my cheeks at the injustice of our situation.

"What will it be like for our children? We must
      fix this." My eyes lock on Kêhounco,
whose steady presence is made more profound
         with her changing shape.

"Our children must know true freedom. They
      deserve a home, a country where
they belong." The room erupts in a chorus
         of yeses, and for the first time

I believe we will do it. This group—
      who together has endured so much—
we can survive this, too. "We must find a way,"
         I say and take Kossola's hand.

KOSSOLA

IN WHICH WE COME TO A DECISION

When I look around de room, at all these
people I have come to love, I know I'd
do anything for them. Dey deserve it. *We*
deserve it. "We should go to Meaher
and Foster. Dey are de ones who brought
us here. Dey should be de ones to send us
back." Kupollee nods. "It's not fair that
the land transfers don't apply to us. *Our* land
is in Africa. If the government is giving land
back to former slaves, they should give
us our land back, too—by sending us home."
Gumpa nods and shares his experiences
from Ouidah. "It is possible Meaher
and Foster will send us back." But Abilè
shakes her head. "No," she says. "What good
are Meaher and Foster? What good have
they ever brought us?" She stomps her foot. "No,
we can't expect anything from them. They will
only disappoint us. We must do this ourselves."
De room falls silent, because Abilè is right.
We just don't want her to be right. We want
magic. A miracle. We want *justice*.

GUMPA
THE PLAN TO PURCHASE PASSAGE

"We must deny ourselves everything except what we need," I announce.

"Work more hours at the mill, take more trips to Mobile to sell our produce."

Kupollee looks to the women. "If this is going to work, then you women must resist purchasing fine fabrics, no matter how it catches your eye."

Kêhounco rolls her eyes, then points a finger at all us men. "The same rules go for all of you as well!"

I swallow and stare down at my shiny new shoes.

I do love wearing nice footwear; it is my weakness.

It will be difficult to abstain from this, but I am determined.

The women link arms, and I suppress a grin as Kupollee throws his hands up in surrender. "Sorry," he says.

I lean over and whisper into Kossola's ear, "If only James were here. These women are too strong for us."

He flashes a grin. "That is de truest thing I have heard all day. Though, if James were here, we still would be no match for them."

The room relaxes into laughter as we enjoy a brief respite from our longing.

KÊHOUNCO
NEW REALITY

When I look around the circle, I miss James's face, his braids.

"If we go back," I tell Abilè, "the baby will never know her father." I'm sure it's a girl by how low she sits. "I'll be alone." Because I know James won't go with us.

"Alabama is James's home," I say. "He doesn't want to go to Africa."
Abilè puts an arm over my shoulders. "Maybe he'll change his mind."
I shake my head. "No matter." With James in the army, I'm already alone.

JAMES

OCTOBER 1865

I've been serving the
Union for six months so far.
I have nothing to
show for it except swarms of
mosquitoes covering me

like a blanket while
being stuck in the muck as
I try to trudge my
way through the long backwaters
of Virginia. My body

is a vessel of
viruses. Like I'm just a
slave again—except
in this circumstance I'm owned
by the US government.

I still haven't learned
to read or write yet. "You must
be patient" is all
I ever hear back. Maybe
I should have been more patient,

not rushed off to join
the Union Army, leaving
Kêhounco and our
baby. I hope I haven't
made a horrible mistake.

TIMOTHY

CHECKMATE

I'm teaching Augustine the fine intricacies of chess
on this glorious Sunday morning. It's rare I get a chance
to spend some time with my son. "The key to this
game," I tell him, "is to always be many steps ahead
of your opponent." He's not even in school yet,
but I tell you, he gets it. I'm seconds from calling checkmate
when Cudjo walks into the yard, his shoulders sagging,
a frown on his face. I could shoo him away
like a horsefly, but I'm feeling charitable. "What do you
want, boy?" I ask. His reply is a garble of words
I can barely understand. When are these monkeys
going to lose their accents? "You want my help?" I say to clarify.
"You want to go back to Africa?" My mind
flashes to news of the American Colonization Society,
which takes free blacks and ships them to Liberia at no charge.
That's one way to cleanse this country: ship all those slaves—
I mean *ex*-slaves—away. But it's not my job
to educate Cudjo. "Sounds like a personal problem to me."
I lift my eyebrows at Augustine, return my attention to our game.

AUGUSTINE

CHESS

Call me a silly little boy, but I see what my father's doing.
He acts like Cudjo is a pawn in his own private game—
except even pawns are worth more. Whenever Cudjo
speaks, Father never truly listens. But I do.
Seems to me my father plays by his own made-up rules.

KOSSOLA

DE WAY IT IS

At first it seems impossible—how can
we save any money for passage to Africa
when we make so little? "One dollar a day
at de shingle factory," I say to Abilẹ.
"Ten dollars a month for rent, beef at fifteen
cents a pound, got to have clothes for working.
Doesn't leave much." Abilẹ stops her
humming. "Each little bit will add up. We just
got to keep at it." Delight climbs into
my throat and comes out in a laugh. I like seeing
Abilẹ happy and determined. "You been listening
to Gumpa," I say. Abilẹ cuts her eyes at me.
"Gumpa must say those things about thrift
because he needs to hear it himself.
I've seen his eyes light on a pair of shiny
shoes." My laugh comes from deep in
my belly then. "You're right about that, Abilẹ.
You're right about most everything."
And that's de way it is with us.
We encourage each other. No better
woman in de world, I promise you that.

ABILẸ
WORKING TOWARD AFRICA

With our new goal in mind, our lives fall into
　　　　something of a routine. Kossola rises at dawn
and sets off walking to the shingle mill with only
　　　　　　a slice of bread dotted with molasses.

I join Kêhounco and the other women in the garden,
　　　　　where we plant and tend greens, peas, sweet
potatoes, and corn. We sing together and share our dreams
　　　　　　of returning to Africa. No whites in sight.

At night, after a single slice of bread for supper, Kossola
　　　　　and the other men make baskets out of oak boughs.
They soak the strips of wood, then weave them into shape.
　　　　　　Once the baskets are dry, we fill them

with the crops. As Kêhounco's belly grows heavy and tight,
　　　　　we walk door to door, offering our produce
for sale. Three days a week we carry the vegetables.
　　　　　　Three days a week we come home,

our pockets jangling and our baskets empty. Every
　　　　　coin that goes into the pot brings us closer
to each other, and to Africa. I learn I'm happiest
　　　　　　when I take my fate into my own hands.

TIMOTHY
CIRCLE OF CONFUSION

My dead relatives would be spinning in their graves
if they could see how these darkies disrespect
us white people today. I try to get my ex-slave
Bridget to milk my oxen during an afternoon
rain shower, and she says, "You have two hands,
milk her yourself." It takes everything in my body
not to grab a whip and give her the peeling of
the century. Although if I did—and I would tell
no one else this—she'd probably start hitting me
back, and I wouldn't want to suffer those blows;
she's as stout as a Birmingham mule.

What is the world coming to?

JAMES

FEVER DREAM

Our weary troops are
dropping to their deaths faster
than pigeons during
trap-shooting. I'm hanging on
by half a thread. Instead of

being treated in
a hospital, I'm taken
care of in a swamp.
I'm having fevered visions
of Kêhounco cradling me,

whispering, "Come home
to your family. We need
you, my sweet, strong man."
Her words will be my North Star
leading me back to Mobile.

For now, though, I march
from state to state through rubble,
wetlands, and the air
of death to help broken souls
rebuild their communities.

I pour myself in
this work while also making
sure to extinguish
any lawlessness that might
flare up at any moment.

KOSSOLA

THESE DAYS

We work from sunup to sundown.
Most nights, when Abilẹ and I
finally lay our heads down, we collapse
into sleep. We stay focused on our
goal—maybe too focused. We don't linger
on de everyday happenings, like how
people look at me strange and ask, "Where
are you from? What's wrong with your teeth?"
Black-skinned or white, most treat me
like I'm part of de traveling circus. I don't tell
them much, just smile and laugh. Can't blame
them for being curious. But some carry
storms in their eyes, like Meaher and Foster.
We hear stories all de time about women
being hurt real bad, raped, even killed
sometimes. Makes my breath come easier
knowing Abilẹ is a home wife—not out
in de world working alone. "You stay with
Kêhounco," I tell her. "Keep together."
Fear streaks across her face, bright
as summer lightning. But then she pushes
her shoulders back. "Nothing bad will happen,"
she says. "That's behind us now."
I've learned not to argue with Abilẹ.
And so, happiness finds us. We may be
busy, but now we're de boss of our own lives.

KUPOLLEE

BROKEN PROMISES

We use newspapers to teach ourselves
to read. I take to it quickly—
I excel at languages.
An article about
the Freedmen's Bureau
pledges forty
acres for
each black
man.

My shipmates get all charged up with hope,
but I know better. I'm not shocked
when President Johnson flips
the law, giving that land
back to white former
Confederates.
"Africa,"
I breathe.
Soon.

TIMOTHY
I DON'T BELIEVE MY EYES

Foster and I are smoking cigars after a meeting
when we see a group of darkies dressed in military
uniforms marching down the street, each looking
crisper than a starched shirt, with faces as proud as you
please. If that's not enough of a sight to behold, what
really gets my heart ratcheting is what they're
carrying—bayonets and muskets.

Good God.

I go into boss mode. "Get home to Adelaide," I tell Foster.
"Now, more than ever, we must protect what's ours."

GUMPA

CONVENTION OF COLORED PEOPLE

Kossola and I sit in church pews, surrounded by black people.

Except for how everyone is dressed, we could be back home in Africa—even though we are in Mobile at the Convention of Colored People.

So many people in one place puts me on high alert.

Not Kossola—his face offers warmth and welcome to others as we listen to the speakers' words.

On this day, November 22, 1865, we pledge to ourselves, our families, and our communities that we will extend harmony and altruism to our white inhabitants and hope to be extended the same courtesy.

These words please me, as I am not interested in being part of a rebellion—I wish only to be treated as a human being.

Still, we must demand fair pay and not give up our newly won rights.

Kossola and I both join in the wild applause.

However, I cannot stop thinking of how there is talk, and there is action—and sometimes one does not correspond with the other.

KÊHOUNCO
MOTHERHOOD

Abilẹ̀ is with me when my baby boy is born. I call him Jerry—an easy American name.

Jerry wants only to be close to me, so I make sure we are always touching. The warmth of him sinks right through my skin into my soul.

By the time he is two months old, the world changes again: "All troops discharged," Abilẹ̀ tells me. I suck in my breath. "James." He'll come home soon. He'll meet his son. "Your daddy's coming," I tell Jerry, and I swear he smiles at me.

JAMES

JANUARY 5, 1866

I start this new year
feeling fresher than morning
dew because today
I'm leaving the army. What
a waste of nine months! Never

moved up in rank or
earned good wages. I'm tired of
being infirm from
marching through those insect-filled
backwaters. Yes, I learned to

read, but never had
the time or funds to grasp how
to write. If I had,
maybe I could have become
more than a private. Doesn't

matter. I soon head
out for Mobile, pockets filled
with one hundred bucks
in bonuses. I'm going
home to Kêhounco at last!

KÊHOUNCO

REUNION

I know it's James by the way he strides toward me with energy and purpose.

My breath comes fast as he sweeps me and Jerry into his arms. "You're here," I say, into his neck. "Yes," he says. "And who is this?"

His fingers stroke Jerry's cheeks as I introduce them. Then his palm finds my cheeks. "I missed you," he says. Tears come to my eyes because I realize that I truly love him. I hug him tight. "Don't ever leave me again."

JAMES

MOMENTARY HAPPINESS

I rock Jerry in
my arms. Feels like he's sunshine,
radiating health
and peace. I sigh, thankful my
little family is at

last in the same room.
When Kêhounco grabs my hand,
whispers her wish to
circle back to her motherland, I listen. "You would love

it, James. There's no white
people to hurt us. Our skin
color is looked on
with respect. We're the rulers
of our own destiny." I

stare off, lost in thought.
Here we are black first, our pride
tossed out like table
scraps. "Okay, my sweet," I say.
"I'm interested." She smiles.

After a few short
hours spent in the loving warmth
of my family,
I leave in search of work. I
find it on a steamboat. My

name—according to
these white men—is still "Boy." I
have no respect for
them, either, but I answer
with a loud, hearty "Yessir."

KÊHOUNCO

APRIL 1866

I put Jerry in his cradle, same as every night, but when dawn comes, he doesn't cry.

I touch his face, but Jerry doesn't move. His skin is cold and blue. When I scream, James comes running. But there's nothing we can do. Our baby is dead.

I hold his body close to me all day. I show him the dogwoods in bloom, the azaleas. I whisper to him about the birds building their nests. I take his body to Abilẹ, and we sing all the counting songs. None of it saves him. I cry for days.

JAMES
OUTSIDER THOUGHTS

I try to press the
death of my son out of my
mind for a while so
I don't injure myself. I
think of another issue.

I don't say this out
loud, yet it's clear to me the
Africans' chances
of going home are as good
as dirt roads turning into

streets of gold—because
there's not enough money. I
can hear Africa's
call now, clear as a bugle.
Somebody, please hear our cries.

GUMPA
ÈSÚSÚ

Tonight at our weekly meeting I notice hours have dissipated like smoke from a campfire as talk centers upon the possibility of going home.

When I suggest the African tradition of an èsúsú, everyone's ears perk up, and their eyes get as alert as hyenas'.

"We would save our money and send just one person back to Africa, and that person would alert all the families and those in neighboring villages, and then they would assemble *their* money to gradually bring all of us back home, one at a time."

My heart rattles as the room fills with conversation, for we may yet find a way to return ourselves to Africa, where we belong.

KOSSOLA

DE STORY OF OUR LIVES

It makes sense to send one at a time
back to Africa. I understand what
Gumpa's suggesting. But one look
at Abilẹ and I know I can't. I promised
I would take care of her, and I don't want
to be without her. "We can't be separated,"
I tell de group. Me and Abilẹ are
like two cornstalks grown intertwined.
"We came here together, and we
should leave together." Maybe it
doesn't make sense from a monetary
perspective, but money isn't everything.
Oluale's de first to nod, and then
everyone's head bobs in agreement.
De days and weeks pass. Before
we know it two years have passed,
and we still don't have enough money.
Still, we keep working
and saving and carrying our slice of
bread dotted with molasses each morning.

WILLIAM

CITIZENSHIP

A quarter century I've lived in this country.
Don't know why I've put off making my
citizenship official. Maybe it was laziness
or being too busy piloting ships. In any
event, I never felt like I needed a piece

of paper to prove I'm American. But today's
news about these filthy congressmen
trying to pass Reconstruction has lit a fire
under me so hot, even Satan himself would
be frightened to look at the flames.

It's so repugnant, I almost hold my nose
when reading about it in the paper.
I'm ready to run to the local court so I can
become a citizen. My right to vote
will hopefully help bring our country

back to its former glory. While Canada's
my heart, this country is my soul.
For all it's done for me, the least I can do
is to join the fight for white dominance.
I now bleed the colors of America's flag.

KOSSOLA

BECOMING A CITIZEN OF DE UNITED STATES

Even though de Fourteenth Amendment
makes former slaves like James
and Noah citizens of de United States,
de law doesn't apply to us—because
we weren't born in America. "What about us?"
I ask Gumpa. "We must go and get
citizenship ourselves," he says.
Typical Gumpa, he is not one to stand
by, but instead charges forward. It takes
three months, but eventually, in October 1868,
de time comes for a group ceremony
at de courthouse where we join others like us,
but not like us. We all have different stories,
but dey all start with us being born in another
country. "State your name, age, and how
long you've been in America," de clerk says.
I give them my American name, not my
African one. "Been here ten years," I say,
so that's what de clerk writes down.
It's not until our walk home that I realize
I've made a mistake. "*Eight* years," Kupollee
says, shaking his head. "Took us eight
years to belong in this country." My eyes
widen. "It's only been eight? I said 'ten.'"
My stomach clenches. "Should I go
back and tell them?" Gumpa shakes his
head. "It does not matter. We are citizens now."

I stare at de certificate with its official
signatures. For once my smile doesn't want
to come. We should be in Africa, not America.
Eight years, and all we've got to show for it
is a thin sheet of paper.

X.

AFRICAN TOWN

JANUARY 1870–FEBRUARY 1885

TIMOTHY

ARTICLE

I make a New Year's resolution in 1870 to work less and
enjoy life more, especially in Mary and Augustine's
company. Instead of spending one day a week with them,
I now spend at least three. It's all about progress.
I even allow both to join me at breakfast more often.
We're each reading pieces of the *Mobile Register* one morning
when an article brings on a fit of laughter. It's about Africans
pleading to return to their homeland—how much they could serve
their people better over there than in America. "What a bunch of
balderdash!" I share the article with my family. Mary laughs as well,
but Augustine's smile is weaker than a worn-down paddle wheel.
What kind of son am I raising?

AUGUSTINE

BALDERDASH

Breakfast would be better if it didn't include us reading newspaper articles. Now that I'm almost nine years old, it's harder for me to simply listen to my father's opinions. These days I want to argue, to declare myself. Like today: Why shouldn't the Africans go home? Every one of them left something—or someone—behind.
Really, I would hate it if I couldn't live here at our home on Telegraph Road. Daddy sees things one way, and that's it. But there's no point in arguing. You can't win against my father. So I dig into my plate of scrambled eggs and focus on other things. Should I go fishing today, or hunting? Doesn't much matter, so long as it gets me outside.

JAMES
MOVING ON UP

Time wings away fast
as a red-tailed hawk. It seems
1870
is the year I can at last
see progress. After years of

saving money from
working on the riverboat,
me and Kêhounco
purchase our very own farm.
We keep pigs, chickens for eggs,

cows, horses, and more.
My reading skills help me learn
excellent farming
methods in books. We share food
with those less fortunate, work

side by side. Rarely
argue. There are those who think,
because I'm a man,
I'm responsible for our
successful business. No way.

Kêhounco handles
all our finances. I'm not
my full self without
her strength. She's one tough woman.
I'm one lucky, lucky man.

KOSSOLA
ON DE PASSAGE OF TIME

De years pass quickly. Our son Aleck
is born. Our home's filled with love,
and before I know it, we're into
a whole new decade: de 1870s.
"Never thought we'd be in America
so long," I say to Abilè in de lamplight
as de baby sleeps. She reaches for
my hand, and our rough, calloused fingers
intertwine. "Long time," she says. I nod.
"Too long." We don't talk much about
èsúsú or de money for going back
to Africa. We're all from different places,
and no one wants to go alone—
or leave loved ones behind.
When we go, we want to go together.
We still add our earnings to de pot,
but it feels like it will never be enough.
Each day is full of living and leaves
us weary. I settle in beside her,
do de one thing guaranteed to cheer
us: I tell Abilè a story—a story of Africa.
A story of home.

ABILẸ̀
UNEXPECTED CONSEQUENCES OF MOTHERHOOD

Our son Aleck keep me busy from sunup
        to sundown. I don't mind. I love his
sticky hands and eager mouth. I'm so busy
            tending him that my thoughts

can't linger on what used to be. "I'm not sure
        about putting a baby on a ship,"
I confess to Kossola. Our own journey was
        so miserable, it frightens me

to think of putting a child through it. Kossola
        doesn't try to cheer me like usual. Instead
he gets quiet. "I don't know if I could find my
            way back to Bantè. What if

I can't remember de way?" His brow creases, and all
        I want to do is smooth it. "You'll remember,"
I tell him. He goes to the money pot, starts
            counting. "We're never going to

have enough," he says. "Not for all of us."
        I slap the baby's burp cloth at his leg.
"Not if we keep having babies, that's for sure."
            He rewards my efforts with a grin,

and I relax into my chair. "Sometimes," he says,
        "I think we should just accept that we're
here to stay. We're never going to get back to Africa.
            Not this year. Not in five years. Not ever."

TIMOTHY
DINNER TALK

I'm celebrating with some businessmen, tucking into
barbecued ribs, fried okra, and cornbread while downing
it all with beer colder than an Alaskan's tears in winter.
One of the men, William Turner, has twice as much
money as I do from his sawmill. Yet he keeps curling his lips
in jealousy every time somebody stops by and pats
my shoulder instead of his. All thanks to winning the bet
that brought those Africans over to this country.
"Losing slave labor must have lightened your pockets
a little, eh?" Turner says. What a poltroon.
I shake my head. "I don't need slaves to be successful.
They were a garnish at my house of plenty—like caviar
during appetizers, asparagus during dinner, or thin slices
of chocolate cake for dessert. Our family will continue
to do just fine financially, thank you very much."
One of the other men, J. Wellington Seibert, who's also
in the shipping business, says, "Obviously, you're doing
fine, Tim. You may be retiring from your shipping work,
but I can't afford to leave my business yet."
I smile. I always liked him. "Well, Seibert, truth is I'd rather
retire than allow anyone of color to be given cabin privileges on
a ship of mine." For once, mine and Turner's not-so-friendly
competition is snuffed out as laughter cascades from our table.

KOSSOLA
NEW IDEA

I don't know how de idea first comes to me.
I wake one morning, and there it is:
"If we can't go back to Africa," I tell Abilè,
"we should use our money to buy land.
Make our own town." Her eyes widen,
and her always-moving mama-body
goes still. "Make our own Africa?" she says.
I nod. "Sure. As best we can." Her cheeks
lift. "Our own town. I like it." When I share
my idea with de group at our next meeting,
dey are all smiles and bright eyes.
"We need a leader," Kêhounco says. "A king."
None of us is a king, and only one of us
comes from noble blood. "Gumpa,"
Kupollee and I say in unison. De room
fills with sighs and soft laughter. Of course.
Gumpa's de only choice. He was de one
to soothe people on de *Clotilda*.
He was de one who made sure all received
water. Kupollee faces Gumpa. "What say you,
Gumpa? Will you be our king?"
I hold my breath. After a long moment,
Gumpa stands, bows before us. "Only if it is
unanimous," he says. It makes sense to vote.
"So let it be done," I say, remembering
my ìyá's decisiveness when my parents
discussed my readiness to marry.
"May de spirits of de elders guide us."

KÊHOUNCO

VOTE

So what if Gumpa is from Dahomey, where our lives were taken from us?

So what if he's Fon, when most of us are Yorùbá? The serpent tattooed on his son Leroy's chest is proof of his devotion to our homeland.

Gumpa is the only one of us of noble birth. He also suggested the èsúsú. Even though it didn't work, it shows his dedication to us, and to Africa. As we cast our votes, my heart is sure it will be unanimous. And it is!

GUMPA

REPARATIONS

A hush settles over the room as my fellow Africans await what I am going to say about our next steps.

To be named a leader of this proud group is an honor that humbles me to my bones, and I am certain my life has led to this moment of deep responsibility.

I thank my ancestors from Dahomey for giving strength to my spirit, blazing this path.

Their daily, silent calls to me for continued elevation of self are richer than the rivers of blood coursing through my veins.

"After giving it much thought, the one word that carries more weight for us as a people than any other is 'reparations.'"

I continue to allow my words to come out slow and proper, the way all royal children are taught to speak.

"We were shipped here by the Meahers, against our will, worked to the point of near death, treated like subhuman creatures.

"If we cannot escape this exile, then we are owed land to build our own community, to take our African customs and apply them in this country among ourselves."

"Only one of us can ask the Meahers, and I believe that person, Kossola, is you.

"Your kind, yet strong nature may make it easier for that white man to listen."

As the room fills with "aye" and "yes" and "béèni," my heart swells for my people.

KOSSOLA

SPOKESPERSON

De group wants *me* to have de talk
with Meaher? Yes, I was de one
to ask Captain Tim to hire us
after de war, but that was five years ago.
My stomach clutches.
It'll be one of de most important
talks of my life. De future of all our
children is at stake. "Just smile at him,"
Abilè says. "That's how you won me."
I know she's just trying to help ease
my nerves. "It needs to be de just-right
moment when I talk to him. Better if
he's in a good mood." I pace as I practice
what to say. It's land, after all. In Africa,
land is free. And we've never asked
for help before. Ever since de war,
we've made our own way. "It's not like
it would be money coming out of his pocket,"
I say. Giving us acreage is de least
he can do for what he stole from us.
Businessman that he is, surely he'll prefer
giving land over de cost of passage
back to Africa. Besides, de land
we have in mind sits way out past
Three Mile Creek. What good is that
land to anybody? "I'll be firm," I tell Abilè.
Though I have my doubts.

Land seems to mean something
different in America than in Africa.
Still, de group has asked this of me.
So, I bide my time, watch, and wait.

TIMOTHY
POCKET OF TIME

It's good for a Southern swashbuckler to take
a well-earned pocket of time out of his day to sit
on his plantation and enjoy the scent of honeysuckle
and peach blossoms. Makes a man thankful to be alive.
As the bees and chickadees fill the air with their music,
I notice Cudjo looking as if the world has fallen on top of his
head like an anvil. Mindful of his ax, I sit myself down
on the very log he's chopping. His ax slams into the log
as I pull out my pocketknife and start whittling. "Don't
mind me," I say. Cudjo strides around to face me,
like he's a king of something. "Captain Tim, we need to talk."

KOSSOLA

STANDING UP TO CAPTAIN TIM

Captain Tim doesn't even look up
from his whittling. "What's on your mind,
Cudjo?" This man, this whittling white man
has what we want, what we *need*.
My face warms, and my throat tightens.
I call on de strength of de elders.
"Reparations," I say. As de word
comes out of my mouth, it becomes
realer to me. Even though Captain
Tim's face turns red and stormy, I still
think we have a good case. Unlike
American former slaves like James
and Noah, who've never been landowners,
we come from farms and homes.
We've lost all of it—because of *him*.
We've been robbed not once, but twice.
And it's Captain Tim who masterminded
and financed de theft. He's de one
who carries most of de blame. Yes, Captain
Foster's de one who bought us and near
about killed us on de *Clotilda*. And yes,
Captain Tim's brothers Burns and Jim
worked us, whipped us, and chained us.
But de one in charge is Captain Tim.
I swallow hard, pushing down my fear.
Confronting him is like being a termite
in de path of an elephant. "You," I say.
"You owe us."

TIMOTHY
RESPONSE

Anger surges through my body faster
than being lit with nitroglycerin. "You've got a lot of
nerve, you ignorant fool!" I shout. "I treated you mighty
good when you all were my slaves, like members of
my own family in fact, and this is the thanks I get?
Boy, you listen to me, and listen as loud and clear
as a church bell ringing on Sunday morning—
you ain't entitled to a blessed thing!" I pause to keep
my voice from carrying to the next county, take a deep
breath, and end our conversation by whispering,
"If any of you want any land from me, you'll have
to pay for every last cent of it yourselves."

ABILẸ

NOT DEFEATED

When Kossola walks into the house,
       I am singing counting songs to little Aleck.
I know by the slump of my husband's shoulders
          what has happened.

"Come," I say, and he lays his head
       against me, tells me everything.
"I failed," he says. "How can
          I tell de group that we are still chained?"

He heaves a big breath. "This country is not
       de same as Africa," he says.
"We should fly free as birds in an endless
          sky. But it is not to be."

Beside us Aleck rolls and tumbles like a lion
       cub. "It's not your fault, Kossola. Just means
we've got to find another way." I want to cheer him
          the way he always cheers me.

"Aleck," I say. "Come find your bàbá's smile."
       I stroke Kossola's head as our son plasters
him with sticky hands. Land or no land, I want more babies.
          "We will find another way."

GUMPA

CALL TO ARMS

This evening at our weekly gathering, it is up to me to uplift and inspire.

"Let us anoint our future property as already being our land," I say, "and our words will speak it into existence."

Chins lift and eyes brighten.

I propose to the group that although we already rent property from Captain Timothy, eventually we need to own it.

"Also, we must be strategic and conduct business with other white people who are interested in selling pieces of their land."

Some worry that it will take too long, but I remind them we survived the *Clotilda*, slavery, and war.

"Yes," I say. "It will take time, but it can be done."

I am pleased when others jump into the conversation.

"Let us be determined," I say in a moment of silence.

"However, let our efforts not steal the joy from our lives."

Land is secondary to the importance of those with whom we share it.

KÊHOUNCO
HOW OUR GARDENS GROW

If anything, Captain Timothy's refusal fuels our desire to improve our lives.

Even though James and I already have a place, we want to help purchase more land for everyone. James and the other men get very good at weaving baskets.

We women care for the children and turn even the tiniest scrap of ground into vegetable gardens. We sell our produce door-to-door with smiles that say, *This may be good for you, but it's even better for us.*

GUMPA
THE FALL SEASON OF 1872

As I told everyone two years ago regarding our destiny to own property, and lots of it: "It can be done; we must press on."

Today, our *pressing on* makes a statement to Captain Timothy with as much force as a ship running aground.

Kossola buys land from the Wilsons, a white family in town, and then less than a month later, Kupollee and Ausy purchase property from the Meaher family.

Some of these whites may have evil in their hearts; still, they are not above doing business with us.

They may not like the color of our skin, but they do love the color of our money.

It is a fact: Now we own multiple tracts of land adjacent to each other.

Let no one argue about our right to be in this country.

KOSSOLA

THIS LAND IS OUR LAND

No one is prouder than me on de day
we lay down our money for our own
pieces of land! Let other former slaves
rent from de Meahers, but not us.
"All because we worked together," I say
to anyone who'll listen. We divide
de land just like in Africa—a plot for
each family. We purchase lumber
and nails to start bringing up de first
house. One at a time, de houses pop
up like teeth in a baby's gums. Whoever
de house is for, dey offer eggs or meat
in return for labor, just like back home
when a man would give a cow and palm wine.
I sleep so hard after those long days,
but it's an honest, satisfied sleep.
We may not be back in Africa, but
we're building something all our own.

ABILẸ̀
OUR HOUSE

At first, we all want to build round, adobe
   homes, like the ones we grew up in.
But it isn't practical in America. In Alabama
     most houses are square and made of wood.

Ours is shaped like a rectangle, with two
   rooms and a chimney. Kossola cuts
the logs himself and mortars them with a mixture
     of sand and lime. No cold air creeps in.

Our small family stays warm and snug during winter
   and just about roasts during summer.
When Kossola tells me he wants to build a fence,
     I think it will be made of white pickets,

like we've seen in Mobile. But that's not all
   he does. He fences our house all around
and puts in eight gates. "Not for protection," he says.
     "To remind me of home."

KOSSOLA

WELCOME TO AFRICAN TOWN

Not many folks get to name a town,
but we do. There's no argument about it—
we call it African Town. African is what
and who we are. It's a name that makes sense.
A town far enough from Mobile that it feels
like de center of de world, but also separate
from de world. Most folks don't know of it,
so nobody much comes around, except ourselves.
Only white folks we see are de Meahers,
who live not far away, and sometimes Foster.
We spend our days working in de white world,
but when we come home, there's no one to poke
fun or ridicule or ask ignorant questions about
my marks or my chipped teeth. Truly, in African
Town, we can simply be ourselves. As de years
pass, our families keep growing, expanding.
Abilè and I welcome our second son and call him
Cudjo, Jr. With his loud cry, he will not be
ignored. We are not surprised when he goes
straight from sitting to walking. Oh, how I love
seeing our town full of children! And I love
whenever an American marries into our town,
because it makes us a more solid community—
more like Bantè. "Welcome," I say, spreading
my arms wide. "Welcome to African Town."

KUPOLLEE

FOR THE LOVE OF FARMING

It's not Africa, but African
Town gives me dirt to press seeds in—
two acres beside the house
to grow what pleases me.
Sun and rain bring life.
My green thumb
is still
green.

KÊHOUNCO
OUR WAY

If it was just me, I might live in African Town. But James and I are a team—

and he doesn't want to live there. "I like living in Mobile," he says. Because he's not African. "Okay," I say, not because he's the boss; because I want him happy.

"You'll always belong here, whether you live here or not," Abilè reassures me. But when I tell her we share our money, even what I earn selling produce, her brow wrinkles. "That's not the African way," she says. "No," I say. "But it's *our* way."

ABILẸ

THE CHALLENGES OF PARENTHOOD

It's true I'm busy with my own family—
        so busy! African Town gives us a safe place
to raise our children, but it can't bring back
           our mothers or sisters.

So much falls into our laps to handle, without
        any help whatsoever. Which is why it's hard
having Kêhounco even three miles away.
           I want her closer than that.

But she has her own life to live. And Kossola
        and I have the children—Aleck and Cudjo, Jr.,
always squabbling with each other, climbing and falling
           and breaking things. Even Kupollee, who passes

no judgment on anyone, tells Kossola that we need to
        rein the boys in. "They need more discipline,"
he says. "So they'll be prepared for the world out there."
           He means the world outside of African Town.

I don't disagree with him; I just don't know what to do.
        There isn't time, and as uneasy as my stomach
has been, I suspect we will soon add another child
           to our family. Perhaps this time it will be a girl.

KOSSOLA

GETTING TO KNOW GOD

Sure as de grass grows out of de earth,
Free George shows up near every day
around African Town, determined as de sun
to drop light even through de thickest brambles.
He shares de Bible with us, and he's quick
to pick up a broom or a hammer. Whatever
we need help with, he's willing to lend a hand.
Yes, Free George is a true friend to us. And, oh,
how I love to hear those Bible verses!
Especially Psalms. That book with its lovely
passages about de earth and how to live
makes me fat with happiness. So many grand
stories fall out of Free George's mouth
and into my heart that I just want to hear more.
Which is why we join him for services at de Methodist
Church down in Toulminville. My whole body
gets tingly and warm when we sit in those pews
listening to de Word of God. It's not that I
no longer believe in Yorùbá. There's just no orò
here. Whenever I go to church or hear de Bible
stories, I am filled with a sense of warmth,
like I finally belong. It always surprises
me when people question me about whether
I believe in God. Of course I do. Somebody
built de sky. How else could we have survived
all that happened to us? I am first in line
to get baptized, because that's where
I want to go when I die: over yonder,
to de sky, to be with God.

JAMES

THE CALLING

After all this time
listening to Free George talk
about God, now it's
happened, just like he said it
would. I'm overwhelmed with joy.

It's as if God threw
thunderbolts of glory from
the heavens into
my heart. There's no other way
to describe it. Instead of

being a former
soldier for this country, I'm
now permanently
part of God's army. My wife
hasn't felt the calling yet,

so I ride to First
Congregational Church by
myself with a love
of God that burns brighter than
a sky overwhelmed by stars.

KOSSOLA
DE LORD'S PRAYER

One Sunday in church, a preacher
named Phillips visits after he's returned from
twelve years in Yorùbáland—so close to Bantè!
My heart just about swells out of my chest
to hear him speak of it. But that isn't de best
part. De best part is when Reverend Phillips
says de Lord's Prayer: He speaks
not in English, but in Yorùbá. To hear de
familiar words, our own language, falling
off his lips—it's as if God himself
is stretching his hand out and inviting us
to climb into his palm. I leap out of de pew
when he finishes de prayer. All of us Africans
shout and cry, we are so full of de Holy Spirit.
At de end of de service, we circle de Reverend
to tell him about ourselves and where
we're from. "We want to go back," I tell him.
"Help us go back." His eyes brighten.
"You should contact the ACS." He tells us
about de American Colonization Society.
"They help people like you get out of the United
States." I about faint to hear of this organization.
"They pay for everything," Reverend Phillips says.
"Some twelve thousand free blacks have already
been shipped home." De very next day,
twenty-six of us shipmates put in our petitions.
In de weeks that follow, I smile all day,
every day, as we wait to hear de news
about when we, too, will be sent to Liberia.

KUPOLLEE
A CHURCH OF OUR OWN

We
soon grow
weary of
walking miles to
Mobile, so we save
money, gather supplies
to construct our own building.
Waiting to hear from ACS
is tough, but working makes us happy.

No
one helps
more than Free
George. Our shipmate
Rose also keeps close
to me. She likes gardens
and growing green things—like me.
I impress her with my many
languages. Love grows in this rich soil.

KOSSOLA

PROMISE

Two years pass, and we don't hear
back from de ACS. "Why do dey
ignore us?" I ask Reverend Phillips.
"Twelve years we've been in this country.
Twelve years! We just want to go home."
Reverend Phillips shakes his head, says
maybe there's been a mix-up. He clasps
my hands. "Maybe God has other plans for you."
I don't want to believe him. I don't want
to give up. So de reverend writes a letter
to de ACS for us, asking them to send us home.
Each day I get through my work by thinking
a letter will be waiting when I return to de house.
Each night I go to sleep believing de letter will
come de next day. But de letter never comes.
It's Abilè who shakes me out of my stupor.
"Where is the man I married?" she asks.
"Bring him back, the one who smiles and laughs.
The one who loves the world." I pull her to me,
hug her hard. She smells of sunshine
and milk. She's what's real. "No more waiting,"
I promise her. "From this day forward
I will be here, now, with you."

ABILẸ

OLD LANDMARK BAPTIST CHURCH

Nobody's happier than me on the day
      the church is finished and we walk
over for our first service. The building sits
      right next to our house,

just past the picket fence with the eight
      gates. It isn't anything fancy, which
is part of why I love it. Just a simple white
      clapboard building, with a foyer

and windows on nearly every wall. Sunshine
      streams in as we sing and give thanks
for our good fortune. It's in our church that I feel
      the sense of community I knew in Africa.

It's not that we've traded one religion for
      another. We've simply added a new layer
of happiness. When the service ends
      and we step outside, Kossola

lingers for a moment, staring out past
      the horizon. "Somewhere over there,
that's where our home is." I smile, pleased
      that everyone agreed with his

suggestion to build the church facing east,
      toward Africa. The children tug at our legs.
"Hungry," Cudjo, Jr., says, his face scrunched. Kossola
      scoops him up, carries him home.

JAMES

PARTNERSHIP

After Kêhounco
gets pregnant again, she's hit
by God's thunderbolt.
"James, I'd like to worship at
Old Landmark," she says. "I know

you prefer I go
to your church, but I truly
feel called to them." I
pause, gather my thoughts, then say,
"Being independent in

our faiths while staying
joined in matrimony is
righteous as rainfall
because it's only between
you, me, and our loving God."

While our religious
principles are different,
we still support each
other. At night, when she shoots
out of bed screaming after

another bad dream
from being kidnapped and shipped
to America,
I'm there to hold her. When I'm
sicker than an infected

possum from being
in so many wetlands while
serving my country,
she cradles my head, serves up
homemade potions along with

whispers and kisses.
We even join a grassroots
organization
to pursue reparations.
Yes, Lord, it's time for justice!

KÊHOUNCO
MOVING CLOSER TO GOD

On Sunday mornings I get up before dawn, walk to African Town for church.

People dressed in their finest clothes spill out of doorways, join together on the path. I link arms with Abilè as Kossola and the children move ahead.

We don't dance or shout like at our first church—white people made fun of us for that. At Old Landmark we worship all day, still as a flock of birds resting together in the branches of an oak tree. But, oh, how we sing!

KOSSOLA

DE VISITOR

One steaming day a white man comes poking
around African Town. We get curious visitors
from time to time. This one wants to know
about our church, our gardens, and where
we're from. "Come on in out of de sun,"
I tell him. He sits with me and Abilè, and I
describe Bantè to him. "You must miss it,"
de white man says. "All we want," I say,
"is to go back there. To go back home."
His brow crinkles. "You can't go back
to Africa now," he says. "If you did, you'd
have to give up your religion." I don't know
what to say to that—what is it that
makes people who don't even know us
so sure about our beliefs? I am Yorùbá
and Christian. Both are part of me.
Both make me who I am. In America,
no one can take that from me. While I grind
my teeth, Abilè is all smiles and patience.
She puts a look on that man plumb full of pity.
"God lives in our country, too," she says.
"He finds us wherever we live." I tell you,
that woman could convince de devil
himself. Her words inspire me to share
something else with de white man. "You know
what de biggest surprise is?" I say. "That
God in America also has a son. We didn't
know about Jesus until we came to Alabama."

I tell him about Free George. "He was
de one to tell us. Come around here reading
de Jesus stories in de Bible. How Jesus
turned water into wine and walked on water!
Here in African Town we try to follow
Jesus's example." De white man nods.
"Hallelujah," he says, like he's accomplished
something important. "And soon you'll
cast your first vote." I nod because de vote
is coming up. Abilẹ clatters some dishes,
and I know she's run out of patience.
She doesn't like talking about de vote
because it doesn't apply to her and de other
women—only men. De children save
de day when dey start fussing and wrestling
around. That white man soon makes
his excuses, and I shut de door behind him.

TIMOTHY

POLITICS

I can't believe these state elections. It's 1874,
and you'd think these Republicans have better
things to do than try to legislate for equality.
It's downright unconstitutional.
What is happening to our country?

Here's what I know to be true as sure as oxygen
goes in and out of my lungs. These Africans have no right
to cast their ballot for anything on this earth.

If these mongrels are going to vote, I've got to convince
them to vote for my party! I head over to African Town,
then make my voice gentle as Mary's when she's trying to
coax a cat out of a tree. I say to them, "You don't
know much about politics, but trust me, we Democrats
know what's best for you all. We'll take good
care of you, like we've always done."

Their expressions are more difficult
to read than an empty bank book.

KUPOLLEE
VOTING

Captain Tim's speech only makes us more
determined to vote for our man.
If the Democrats prevail,
life will be worse for us.
Three of us march in
a single line
to cast our
precious
votes.

TIMOTHY
VOTING STATIONS

They walk like a pack of gorillas down
the road, ready to cast their votes. Obviously
they didn't listen to what I said to them earlier.
Looking back on it, when did they ever listen?

From astride my horse I shout, "Who are you going to vote for?"
None of them respond. Anger sends blood rushing
to my head. I scream out, "Don't allow them to cast their ballots!
They're about as American as a boatful of Chinamen!"

My friends at the voting station turn them away.

Now, I know these mongrels better than they
know themselves. Most of them are more
stubborn than a brick wall. I'm positive they'll
go to another voting station—and when
they do, I'll be there waiting.

KOSSOLA

FIRST VOTE

Captain Tim's determination to stop
us from voting only makes us more resolved
to outwit him. He beats us to four different
polling stations—but he has de advantage
of riding horseback while we're on foot.
I'm not sure at first about defying him
by visiting yet another station, because
I still work for de man. "What if he fires me?"
I ask de others. "He won't," Kupollee reassures
me. "You're too good at your job. You show up
even when others don't." That gives me
confidence, because nothing matters more
to Captain Tim than getting as much work done
as quickly as possible. Then it comes to me.
"We've got to go to Mobile to vote. He won't
imagine us going that far." Kupollee, Oluale,
and I join in a circle before we set out.
"God, help us," I say. "Help us cast our votes."
Just before sundown we arrive at St. Francis
Street, our legs weary, but our hearts full.
No Captain Tim in sight. "We're here to vote,"
I tell de white people behind de table.
De white man stands. "Don't you know, boy?
It costs one dollar to vote." We know it's not
true because dey don't tell any of de white
folks that, just us. No matter. We won't be beat.
I bust out my best smile and pull a wad
of cash from my pocket. I peel off a dollar

bill and slap it on de table. De man's face
turns even whiter. He doesn't speak again,
just hands over de ballots for us to fill out.
We take our time walking home—
so proud of ourselves for not giving up,
for letting our actions and our ballots speak.
"They thought they had us," says Kupollee.
"I'd have paid even more than a dollar
to see the look on that man's face."
"Only thing that would've made it any
better," I say, "is if Captain Tim had been
there to witness it."

GUMPA

WHISPERS IN THE NIGHT

At our weekly meeting we speak of our children, of what they need to grow and prosper in this community.

"We have all heard about the school in Mobile for black children only; it is the first of its kind," I say.

"What if we were to build a school for our children, here in African Town?"

The walls vibrate with excitement as a cacophony of "yes" fills the room.

The energy is punctured by the easy voice of Kupollee.

"That school requires constant watching so that white men don't torch it, and the teachers, too."

"I understand your concern," I reply.

"However, the only way to move forward in life is to take chances—like four years ago when we took a chance and voted despite the white man trying to block us from doing so."

"You speak the truth," he responds.

I wait for the room to settle.

"Let us now discuss the where and how of building our own school."

ABILẸ

ON THE NEED FOR SCHOOLING

I am first to jump into the conversation
       about building a school. No one
is surprised—they all know we have five
       boys already, and a new baby

coming any day now. "Our children deserve
       better than what we got," I say. "I don't
want white people calling them 'ignorant'
       like they call us."

Everyone nods in agreement, and I almost
       confess that what I really need is help—
these children wear me out. Time with a teacher
       would also give me a break.

"I want them to know everything," Kossola says.
       "So their lives will be easier than ours."
I grab his hand, grateful again for the way
       he reads me. "We can't wait

for anyone else to do this for us," I say. "It's our
       problem, and we should be the ones to make
it happen." When we return home, Kossola scoops
       Cudjo, Jr., into his arms for a story.

CUDJO, JR.

FREEDOM

my bàbá lifts me onto his lap/ starts telling
me an african story
about ajapa and the fly

i do not care

i twist away/ but his arms are too strong

ihatethis ihatethis ihatethis

i am six years old/ too big to be on bàbás lap

like the horses I see running in the fields

I need to be *f r e e*

KOSSOLA
GOOD TIMES, TOUGH TIMES

We build a school, same as we built
de church. No one's happier than
Abilè on de very first day! Inside de
school a black teacher we hired ourselves
sits at de desk we also built for her. "Mind
your teacher," Abilè instructs de boys
as she snuggles baby Celia to her chest.
Finally, we've got a girl to add to our pack
of boys. Her Yorùbá name is Ebeossi,
which means "no apology necessary."
Her fresh scent and easy smiles help us
get through tough times when de boys get
into one kind of trouble or another. One day,
dey set fire to de field. Another day, dey nearly
drown a litter of kittens as dey attempt
to "wash" them in de river. Neighbors say
dey are too loud, too destructive. Cudjo, Jr.,
loves throwing rocks best of all. More than once
he's broken a window. Sometimes Abilè and I
talk about them in Yorùbá so dey won't know
what we're saying. How I savor de taste
of those sweet, old words in my mouth.

CUDJO, JR.

SCHOOL

my mind likes to tap dance
from one thing to another during school

the voice of my teacher/ miss nottingham
goes silent as i inhale aromas
f l o a t i n g in from the windows

peach blossoms/ grass/ and mud call to me

i also smell my favorite thing/ camellias
from kupollees garden

miss nottingham snaps me out of my daydream
please pay attention/ she says

i try to ignore her/ but like summer mosquitoes
shewillnotgoaway

school is boring/ everyone knows i would rather be outside
learning about nature

why do people expect me to be something i am not

KOSSOLA
WEDDING DAY

We get married on a March Monday,
everything greening up around us.
Abilẹ puts on her best dress, and I step
into de pants that have been mended
de fewest number of times. All six children
wear white shirts, and de air's thick with
birdsong. Kupollee and Rose also marry,
as do Ausy and Annie Keeby—a triple
wedding. We could have married
at Old Landmark, but Abilẹ thinks it best
to go back to Stone Street Baptist Church.
Feels more official that way. De children
squirm beside us as we say our vows
and Reverend Burke blesses our unions.
"You may now kiss your bride," he says,
finally. That's when eight-year-old Cudjo, Jr.,
showers us with kissy noises, so we
hurry out of de sanctuary. I nudge Abilẹ
with my shoulder. "You're stuck with
me now." A smile lifts her cheeks
as we walk home to African Town,
where our family and friends wait.
No one's smile's bigger than de
one on Free George's face to see
us married under de eyes of God.

XI.

LIFE IS BUT A DREAM

FEBRUARY 1885–MARCH 1901

TIMOTHY
LAST MAN STANDING

Time moves faster than bullets from a flintlock,
and at seventy-two, my battered bones are slow to move.
Thanks to the coloreds and their so-called rights,
I've moved my money-making focus to our Mobile Steam
Brick Works and Bay City Lumber Company.
I don't regret it, because our family business is still
doing fine—actually, it's bringing in more money
than ever. The world may change, but this old captain
knows how to roll with the swells. Now my focus is on
educating Augustine so that he can handle the company
when I'm gone. He's a bit too softhearted sometimes
for his own good, but still a sharp businessman like his daddy.
No one's more surprised than me when Augustine comes
with sad news. "Uncle Jim's dead," he says.
I grip the desk so I don't splatter onto the ground.
"Not Jim," I say. Even though Burns died five years
ago, it feels like it happened yesterday—and now Jim?
As Augustine tells me the details, my mind moves
in and out like the tide. The Southern swashbuckler
is the last of the Meaher brothers
left with air in his lungs—barely.

WILLIAM

PALLBEARER

I strain as I help carry the casket of Jim Meaher.
It doesn't seem right that we should be sending
him off to his great rewards. I stifle a potential
sneeze while walking along the grass. I used
to joke to Adelaide that I was so strong I could

lift a ship over my head. Not anymore. Age has
crept up on me like a bandit in the dark. I steal
a glance at Captain Tim. He walks with Mary
beside the casket. No longer a giant, he's hunched
over like Quasimodo. His hair's pale as snow.

His days on this earth are fading. It's true: Time cares
for no one. As for myself, some days I'm no more
useful than a puddle of candle wax. I didn't exactly
become governor. I didn't get famous. I didn't make
mountains of money, either. Yet I married,

own a home, and successfully transported
those slaves on my beloved *Clotilda*. Not bad.
I finally realize it's high time to journal these
experiences. The risk of prosecution has long
since passed, and my memory's still sharp.

I'd like to set the record straight, eradicate those
thumpers Captain Tim's been spewing for years.
He's been snatching credit from me since I went
into business with him, what feels like two lifetimes ago.
I'm finally ready to take credit where it's really due.

KUPOLLEE

WHAT THE BEES TEACH ME

Only thing better than gardening
is tending bees. The hive hums all
day, and nothing tastes sweeter
than my honey. "Because
of my fruit trees," I
tell whoever
will listen.
I give
jars

to everyone in African Town.
"Don't they sting you?" the young ones ask.
"Yes," I say. "But I've known worse."
My mind turns to Glèlè,
the barracoon, the
ship. Slavery.
"What's a quick
little
sting?"

KÊHOUNCO
RUMORS AND GOSSIP

I don't want to tell Abilẹ what I'm hearing about her teenage children, but I do.

If someone said the same about my son Willie or Napoleon, I'd want to know. "They call them savages. They say that Cudjo, Jr., might kill someone someday."

"I know they're wild," Abilẹ says. "American kids call them 'dirty Africans.' They think Africans eat people." She shakes her head. "That's why my sons fight." I start a simple counting song to comfort her, as if we're back aboard the *Clotilda*.

KOSSOLA

FIELDING COMPLAINTS

When a set of parents comes to me
with complaints about our boys fighting,
I don't have any patience for it. Now that
Aleck and Cudjo, Jr., are tall as men,
de problems have gotten worse.
"Your sons provoked them," I say, because
I've already heard this story from my sons.
This could all be so easily prevented.
"Don't you know," I tell them, "if you don't
bother a crocodile, it won't bother you?"
I keep my voice low and gentle, when in truth
I want to shout, "Leave my sons alone!"
Nothing makes me wearier than
hearing all de bad things our children have
done. Thank goodness for our sweet Celia.
She's a happy seven-year-old—strong
like Abilè, and good-natured.
She doesn't get mixed up with others
de way Aleck and Cudjo, Jr., do. She's about
as good at avoiding trouble as de boys
are at stirring it up. "She had to be an angel,"
Abilè says. "God knew we couldn't handle
any more of what we already got." When
her cheeks lift, I'm certain everything will
be okay, if we can get them grown.
"Things will get better," I promise.
Trouble is, I just don't know when.

CUDJO, JR.
I DO NOT BOTHER YOU/ YOU DO NOT BOTHER ME

some people make me wanttoscream
they call me devil/ cannibal/ and baboon
it has gotten worse since my voice is deeper
and i now have chest hair

i do nothing wrong/ i mind my own business

when i do lash out at them with my hands/ they scurry away
faster than scared squirrels/ complain that it is my fault

what cowards

my motto is/ i do not bother you/ you do not bother me
why is this so difficult for people to understand

my parents annoy me/ too/ especially bàbá
he wants me to go to church like he does/
speak yorùbá like he does/ spend time
with our neighbors like he does

that is not who i am

also/ when bàbá gets bullied/ he does not use
his hands to make his point

i do

GUMPA
LAWS

It is hard to believe how many of our children have risen up in height faster than a summer sunrise.

No longer easy babies, they now use foul language, consume various intoxicants, and fail to attend school.

Some have even resorted to theft.

Unacceptable.

So, during our weekly meeting we create the roles of judges for our town.

Ausy and Jaba are chosen—excellent choices.

Both are older than most everyone, and they carry themselves with dignity.

Each of us creates a list of laws.

Among them: *We will not imbibe so much alcohol as to become impaired.*

We will not physically or mentally injure one another.

We will not take possession of items belonging to other people without their permission.

Punishment for anyone breaking the laws will range from a simple verbal admonishment to a lashing.

With each decision, we Africans are becoming even more united.

ABILẸ̀

MOTHER TO SON

The years roll along in Africa Town
        as sure as the ocean reaches from
here to our homeland. 1891 brings surprises
        of one kind and another.

When Aleck comes to us to tell us he wants
        to marry Mary Woods, I am delighted
he's ready for this next step. But I am also
        worried—not because Mary

is just sixteen to Aleck's twenty-four. Mostly
        because she's not one of us. "She's
a second-generation Alabamian," Aleck says.
        "Her grandparents were victims of the slave trade,

just like you." His eyes are bright, and I know
        he needs our encouragement and support,
so I stick to the most important concern. "Is she
        ready to become part of African Town?"

Because that's what marriage to one of us
        means. When Aleck lifts his hand to stroke
my cheek, I am comforted. "Yes, Ìyá. She wants
        us to live here, with you and Bàbá."

I fall in love with Mary in that moment. She and Aleck
        are a fine match. "Well, then," I say, my eyes turning
wet as I imagine the home we'll build for them, right
        here, near ours. "Let's have a wedding."

KOSSOLA
BÀBÁ OF DE BRIDE

Aleck and Mary get married in de fall,
just when de leaves are beginning
to trade their glorious green for gold.
We sing and dance into de night.
Even Cudjo, Jr., is there, his strong hands
creating drumbeats everyone stomps
and twirls to. As firelight illuminates de faces
of my shipmates, I'm aflame with gratitude.
Nothing makes me happier than when
we're all together. When Abilè slips her hand
in mine, I pull her close. "Seems like
no time at all since we were de ones
getting married." She lifts my hand
so that all my scars and swollen knuckles
are revealed. "I'm married to an old man
now." Her white teeth flash against de night,
and I squeeze her to my chest. "Fifty years
since I was born. Doesn't seem possible."
Strange to watch Aleck sway with Mary
and know we are de elders now. "May dey
fill our lives with grandchildren," I say,
and Abilè sighs. "Celia's already starting
to get ideas. Just this morning she told me
she wants her wedding by the river."
I shake my head. "Celia's still a child!
She doesn't need to be thinking about that
quite yet." Abilè tilts her head up at me.
"She's thirteen, Kossola. Not much younger

than when I was kidnapped." I press her
head to my chest. I know she's right, but still,
Celia's our baby girl. "It's different in America,"
I tell her. "I want her to stay a child
as long as possible." But, watching her dance,
even I can see Celia's not a child anymore.

TIMOTHY
MARCH 3, 1892

At age eighty, my body is a prisoner of itself.
These final grains of sand in my life are about
to drop through the other side of the hourglass.

There have been dips, turns, and choppy waters. I've made course
corrections in order to give my family a name to be respected.
My family's built an empire: plantations, vessels, a seaport.

And I led the way.

I've been the captain of the riverboat of my life.
This son of an immigrant from Ireland did all right for himself.
My legacy will stretch on for generations to come.
As Father O'Hara gives me last rites, I muster enough
strength to whisper, "I have no regrets."

KOSSOLA

REFLECTIONS ON DE DEATH OF CAPTAIN TIM

On de day I hear de news, I head for
de river. My insides feel hollow after hearing
about de way dey are glorifying Captain Tim
in de papers for being a successful businessman
and steamboatman. What twists my hat
is how dey give him credit for African Town!
Like he's de one who created it,
when it was our precious dollars, our labor,
our dreams that made this place. Our homes,
de school, de church—dey belong to *us*,
not Captain Tim. I pace along de fence line,
remembering all de ways that man got
in our way. Thank God he's to be buried far from
African Town, in that rich white folks' graveyard
over there in Toulminville. Truth be told,
I'm glad Captain Tim is dead. It's not a Christian
thought, but it's what's real.

ABILẸ
CELIA

We keep Celia close over the next year.
  She's a good girl—responsible and kind.
Which is why I'm surprised one summer morning
    when she doesn't want to accompany me.

"Celia," I say. "Don't be lazy. I need your help selling
  the vegetables. You must come with me."
She sinks into the rocking chair where Kossola
    likes to tell his stories. "I don't feel good."

So she stays home that day and the next.
  Her fever runs so high we run out of rags
to soak and place on her brow. "Call the doctor,"
    I tell Kossola. In all her fifteen years

Celia has never been sick like this. The doctor doesn't know
  what's wrong, but he prescribes medicine. I sit
with her while Kossola goes to fetch it from the drugstore.
    "Your bàbá's coming," I whisper.

I dip the rag in the water bucket, wring it, and stroke
  my baby's hot brow. "Ọ̀kan, èjì, ẹ̀ta, ẹ̀rin,
àrún," I sing. "Please, God," I pray. But none of it works.
    Celia's spirit flies home ahead of us.

KOSSOLA

SAYING GOODBYE TO CELIA

I am de one to coax Abilè away from Celia's
still, cold body. "We must let her go,"
I say, my voice cracking. Such a sweet,
beautiful girl! And now her body is nothing
more than an empty shell. We hold de funeral
at our church, but it's hard for me to look
at her in that open casket. How could God
take her away from us? For what purpose?
Even de Psalms can't bring me any comfort.
While Abilè seems to find some relief in them,
my mouth just won't form de words. It's true
that by now we've lived in America thirty-three
years—longer than we were alive in Africa.
But on this day my heart forgets English. It forgets
Christianity. De words in my head are Yorùbá:
"Àwa ń lọ." We are going away. It troubles me
that Celia should rest so far from our home.
In Bantè we buried de dead within de walls
of de compound in order to protect and keep them
in our lives. De graveyard we built in African Town
is too far down de road. So in de days
after my daughter's body is put into de ground,
I drag out my hammer and nails and cut some
fine pickets. I will protect my daughter's spirit,
keep her close in another way. As I build
de fence around her grave, I sing to her.
I tell her stories. "No need for you to be
lonesome, Ebeossi, I am here."

AUGUSTINE

LITTLE AFRICA

"Let's go," I say when Captain Henry Romeyn, former officer of a Colored
Infantry regiment, asks me to take him to "Little Africa." His experience during
the war makes him interested in black folk. "They call it African Town," I say.
There are other names for it, but I keep those to myself. Sweat trickles down my
legs as the June sun hammers my scalp and we arrive in the clearing
east of Cudjo and Celia's house. "Wow," Henry says,
and it is something to behold: cabins, gardens, children. "They built all this?"
"From the ground up," I say, then zip my lips, not sure if I can trust him with my
real feelings. Keeping quiet is a skill I perfected while my father was still alive.
"I can't believe they own all this and don't just rent," Henry says. "Not like those
country Negroes." I nod. "The Africans are different, that's for sure," I say,
and that's when Gumpa comes out of the woods, striding toward us.

GUMPA

THE CHOICE

Every Sunday afternoon, after some people attend church services in the morning, most of the African men head outside to chop and stack timber.

Sometimes our families join us in our yards, like today, as Abilè hangs clothes with my wife, Josephine.

When we gather like this, I am at my happiest in this country.

Our sense of sanctuary is interrupted when Mr. Augustine rides in with a stranger.

My shoulders hunch.

"This is Captain Henry Romeyn," Mr. Augustine says. "He is interested in knowing more about your town."

Captain Romeyn tips his hat, and I nod, my eyes never leaving his.

"Pleasure to make your acquaintance," he says. "Where did you all originate?"

A chorus of voices, including mine, say, "Dahomey."

"Well," he says, "which do you like better, sir, Dahomey or Ala—"

"Dahomey," I say. "Dahomey, Dahomey, Dahomey."

As I say the words, my lost kingdom appears before my eyes.

ABILẸ
FINDING MY VOICE

Augustine doesn't scare me the way Captain Timothy did,
        so I approach him, my head held high. I know that
if Kossola were here and not with Ausy, fishing in the river,
           he'd at least greet Augustine and this stranger.

"Celia," Augustine says. "Tell my friend Captain Henry Romeyn
        what it was like in Africa." I set down my basket of clothes.
"In Africa," I say, "the land is free. You don't pay tax. You work
           whatever land you please."

Captain Romeyn cocks his head, a confused look on his face.
        "How can you talk favorably about Africa? Wasn't it Africans
who captured you and brought you to America?" Heat rises
           in my cheeks. "That wasn't our people. Those were

criminals. Just bad luck that we got caught up in it." I take a breath.
        "Africa is a good place, a beautiful place. A *free* place."
When the children run past us, stop, and stare, I realize
           my voice has turned as loud and commanding as thunder.

GUMPA

SURPRISE

After Abilè puts this white man, Captain Romeyn, in his place, he says to me, "Well, bottom fact, your kingdom is going through a major upheaval—you do know there are others from Dahomey here in America, don't you?"

I stay as still as an oak.

"No, I did not. How were they captured?"

"Well," he says. "It's been about three years now, but Dahomey went to war with France—and King Glèlè was defeated. Some say he committed suicide."

I am so shocked, the whisper of a breeze could knock me down.

"His son, Béhanzin, survived," Captain Romeyn says.

"He and his soldiers were removed to the Caribbean."

My throat tightens.

I cannot believe my uncle is dead, my cousin's been shipped away—just like me—and Dahomey is lost to the French.

I whisper, "This cannot be true."

"It's true," he says.

I no longer have a home to return to.

KOSSOLA

EVOLUTION OF A DREAM

When Gumpa tells us about de fall
of Dahomey, my heart shrinks a little.
"It is no longer de Africa we were born
to," I say to Abilè. "If we ever did go back,"
she says, "it wouldn't be the same."
I know she's right, but part of me
is still curious. I want to see de changes
for myself, make my own judgment.
But I don't dwell on it. Not with Aleck
and Mary sharing our home. Makes me
proud to have them right here
with us, in our own little compound,
same as it would be in Bantè.
And when Aleck tells me his plans
to get away from shingles and brickwork,
I can't stop smiling for days. "I want
to open a grocery store," he says.
I don't know a thing about being a grocer,
but I know it's a good idea. Everyone needs
groceries. "No more roasting in de Alabama
sun for you," I say and clap him on de back.
"I just want to provide a good life for Mary
and our children," he says. Abilè, who's
at de stove cooking up a stew, starts
singing when she hears those words.
Nobody loves being an ìyá àgbà more than
Abilè! It helps ease some of de hurt
from losing Celia. Doesn't erase it,

but having those children in de house
sure does bring bushels of joy. De only
worries big enough to keep me up
at night are ones about Cudjo, Jr.
"I don't think he's ever going to settle down,"
Abilè says. I grab her hand. "He will,
Abilè. In God's time, not ours."
Oh, how I want my words to be true!
Each night his is de first name
in our list of prayers.

CUDJO, JR.

TRAGEDY

in 1899/ when a goodfornothing black man
named gilbert thomas taunts me

i fight back/ then he fights back

it goes like a boxing match

back and forth
back and forth
back and forth

until i accidentally fan
out the candle of his life

god help me

ABILẸ

NEW YEAR'S DAY 1900

I never imagined we'd be celebrating a new
      year, a new decade, with one child dead
and another detained in the county jail
        on charges of manslaughter.

All those times the neighbors complained
      about the boys fighting, all the times
someone said Cudjo, Jr., would kill someone
        someday, I didn't believe it.

Not my son, I thought. But now he's stuck
      with a bunch of other inmates awaiting
trial. I plead every day for God to keep him
        safe. As I move through my days, I pray:

Please, God, keep Cudjo, Jr., safe. Make this year
      a bountiful one. Bless us and keep us healthy
and safe. In thy name I pray. When Kêhounco
        arrives to accompany me to the trial,

she places a shell in my palm. I gasp. "This is not—"
      She nods, closes my fingers around the shell
she brought all the way from Africa. The one
        she's kept all these years.

"May it bring you comfort. Whatever happens with
      Cudjo, Jr., you always have a home here, with me."
I squeeze the shell, and tears come into my eyes.
        "Thank you, my cheetah-sister."

CUDJO, JR.

VERDICT

time has stuckitselfinmud

less than a week after
jurors are picked/ i am convicted
of first degree manslaughter

sentenced to jail for five years

what shame i have brought
upon ìyá and bàbá

upon african town

there is nothing i can do
to mend this r u p t u r e

what have i done

KOSSOLA

VOW

I can't bear to think of Cudjo, Jr.,
in de penitentiary. If we were in Bantè,
I don't think de orò would have made
de same decision. "You watch," Kupollee
says. "They'll put him in the mines."
That's where all de black convicts go.
"Worse than the *Clotilda*," he adds.
My jaw clenches. If I ever get de chance,
I'm going to tell Cudjo, Jr., more about
what it was like in de hold of that ship.
How we used our minds to survive it,
and how he can do that, too.
"He's strong," I tell Kupollee. "He
has a big heart, and wide, capable
hands." Oh, my son! He didn't ask
for de life he was given any more
than I did. If only I'd been able to get us
back to Africa! Bantè blazes in my
memory, bright and vivid as fireworks.
"Cudjo, Jr., will make it," I say
and pray to God it's true.

CUDJO, JR.

DOCTOR EXAMINATION

i shiver as i stand in line

i think of what my parents went through
when they were auctioned in
africaandamerica

the doctors sweaty hands poke/ pinch/ smear my body

you are a good specimen/ the doctor says softly
his lips s l i g h t l y
brushing against my earlobe

you will do just fine boy/

he winks

i have never felt so dirty in my life

KUPOLLEE

GARDENS OF ONE KIND AND ANOTHER

When
my Rose
dies, I eat
only mush for
days. I am fifty-
one years old. A father
to five. Too young, and too old.
I weep for Africa, my home.
I retreat to my garden, to dirt.

Soon
Lucy—
daughter of
shipmates Sam and
Abache—becomes
my new wife. We grow our
family as easy as
peas in the garden. "Come inside,"
she says when the sun drops. But I stay.

CUDJO, JR.
PRISON JOB

i work in the mines

i am rented out for a monthly fee of ten dollars

twelve hours a day/ i chop and blast out
massive amounts of natural coal
s e p a r a t i n g any bits of rock found in it

the shaft is so small/ i cannot stand upright

all day toiling in bare feet

if i do not do my job right/ i am forced to take off
my pants/ lie on my stomach
as the prison guards whip me

the coal dust is so thick it clogsmythroat

this is killing me

KÊHOUNCO
KEEPING OUR CULTURE ALIVE

Sometimes Abilè visits me in Mobile, and sometimes I go to African Town.

Kupollee, his wife, Lucy, and their kids join us. When we lapse into Yorùbá talk, the children laugh at our strange words. They haven't learned the language.

"All it will take is one more generation before our African ways will die," I tell them. Kupollee nods, but Lucy shrugs in her American way. "We must teach them," I say. "They may be the ones to return to Africa. They need to remember their roots."

CUDJO, JR.
HAIL MARY

when i speak with my lawyer edward m robinson
words t u m b l e out of my mouth

getmeoutofhereplease
getmeoutofhereplease
getmeoutofhereplease

he says/ cudjo jr/ i am doing all i can
thank goodness you did not kill a white man
or else it would have been much worse

i will reach out to people in good standing
in mobile to hopefully sign an appeal
for governor johnson to have you pardoned

i look in mr robinsons eyes and say

i cannot live like this

every night/ i make a silent plea to
my yorùbá ancestors for strength and grace
to survive this madness

AUGUSTINE
PETITION

"Petition for the Pardon of Cudjo Lewis, Jr." are the words
emblazoned at the top of the legal document handed me by
the lawyer Edward M. Robinson. "You think it will work?"
I ask. "Perhaps," says Robinson. "He's a young man." I
take the pen in my hand, scribble my signature without a blink.
"I know the Lewis family. They're honest and hardworking.
Odd, yes, but I respect what they've built for themselves." There's
not much I can do without family approval, but I can sure sign my name.

CUDJO, JR.
WAITING

i follow the tattered calendar every day
inside this cement building of horror

it has been six months so far

when i meet up with mr robinson
his eyesaredancing and his mouth breaks
into a wide g r i n

governor johnson signed your pardon/ cudjo jr

he sticks out his hand for me to shake

you are free

my smile is bigger than the earth

the black letters on my petition blur

so many people in mobile have written
how hard i work/ how i try my best to avoid
trouble/ how respected i am by both black and white people

thank you/ i say to mr robinson

endless combinations of light
shine inside me

i change into fresh clothes/ get a ticket/ arrive back home
where ìyá and bàbá are cutting okra

ìyá screams out ọmọ mi/ my child
she kisses my cheeks

bàbá places his head next to mine/ whispers
welcome home son

KOSSOLA

AN END AND A BEGINNING

I'm just finishing off de pot of coffee
with Cudjo, Jr., when Kupollee comes
walking up de road. "Did you hear?"
he says. "Captain Foster's dead."
I about fall out of my chair. "Are you sure?"
Kupollee nods, his hoops flashing.
"It's in the paper. Lucy read it to me
this morning." I rock back, and de porch
boards creak. "What'd dey say about him?"
Kupollee adjusts his shirt collar against
de February breeze. "Just like when
Captain Tim died. Talking about the *Clotilda*
like it was part of some grand
adventure. Not what it really was."
I lift my pipe from de small side table,
stuff it with tobacco. Take my time striking
de match and drawing in that first suck.
As de tobacco enters my lungs,
something loosens. "He's really dead?"
Kupollee gazes out at de garden, where
collards grow in great green bunches.
"Guess he's going to miss the best
crop of greens we ever did grow."
When I catch Kupollee's eyes,
there's a sparkle in them I haven't
seen in a long while. "I guess so,"
I say, rocking back and sucking
on my pipe. "I guess so."

CUDJO, JR.
FEÏCHITAN AND BÀBÁ

after working at the grocery store/ i find
bàbá sitting in his favorite chair
s t a r i n g out into the copper sunset/ his face
rumpled with sadness

what is wrong bàbá/ i ask

he looks up/ calls me by my african name
oh/ feïchitan/ de ground we walk on
here in america is hard as steel

i wish you could sink your feet
into de soft soil of africa

i am sorry i could not get you
back to de motherland

i curse de men who brought us here

he looks so small sitting across from me/ like a sad turtle

bàbá/ i say/ when i think of captain timothy
and captain foster/ i think of men using
their whiteness to build wealth
on the backs of black people

when i think of the elders of african town/ i see
people who came to this country with nothing

you all created a community
that will be around long after your spirits leave Alabama
your grandchildrens grandchildren and beyond
will make lives on this land because of you

i have never talked this much
at one time with bàbá

a lightningfast smile flashes across his face
before he walks out the door

without a word

CLOTILDA

COMMUNING WITH KOSSOLA

Even from my place under the waves, I recognize the strong
shoulders and easy gait of the one they call Kossola.

For a moment I think he sees me, too. I want to shout: *Speak!
Tell your story! Let me help carry your name across oceans!*

As he paces the shore, I want to be water, not wood—how
I would smooth his troubled brow! How I would like to ripple

against his skin to let him know his life has been a good one.
Despite impossible odds, he and his family of shipmates

have created something beautiful: a home that will anchor them,
even if they never return to Africa. But I cannot be water;

I am only wood. And so I will keep waiting here in the silt until
someone as courageous as Kossola decides to pull me up and listen.

KOSSOLA
COMING HOME

As twilight settles over de trees,
I walk away from de river that first
brought us to Alabama. I ease along
de road, back to African Town, where
de picket fence with its eight gates
welcomes me. De evening air is full
of all de regular sounds: Abilè and Mary
stirring pots in de kitchen, Aleck's voice
booming hello after a long day at de grocery.
From de backyard, an ax-song rises as Cudjo, Jr.,
slices firewood. How his words helped
heal me! And everywhere, de music of our
grandchildren's happy laughter.
Our grandchildren, who are both African
and American. And I know it's time to tell
them everything about me—de whole story.
About Bantè, Glèlè, and de *Clotilda*.
About Captain Foster and Captain Tim.
How I fell in love with Abilè. About slavery
and freedom, and how we made African Town
so dey would know where their home is.
"Come, my children. Let me tell you our story . . ."

AUTHORS' NOTE

This book is a work of fiction. While we have done our best to stay true to actual events, we have taken liberties with personalities, dialogue, and interactions.

When we first learned about African Town (now known as Africatown) while speaking at the Alabama Book Festival in Montgomery, Alabama, on April 13, 2019, we knew this story needed to be brought to a younger audience. We are so grateful for the scholarly works (*see* **Learn More about the Shipmates, the *Clotilda*, and African Town**) that were available to us and have made no attempt to re-create those here. Our purpose was to share this beautiful story of human resilience, heart, and creativity, and to honor those 110 Africans who were captured and brought to Alabama.

Early in our work, Dr. Joél Lewis Billingsley, an associate professor of Instructional Design, Technology, and Human Performance in the Department of Professional Studies at the University of South Alabama, shared with us her commitment to "truthful and triumphant" stories about Africatown. We've kept those words close to our hearts throughout our research, writing, and revising process. We've done our best to gather as much information as possible, to discover the emotional truths, and to convey those truths in this narrative.

As with any historical story, there were gaps in the information available to us, as well as discrepancies among sources. When in doubt, we deferred to *Dreams of Africa in Alabama: The Slave Ship* Clotilda *and the Story of the Last Africans Brought to America* by Sylviane A. Diouf. In her book, Dr. Diouf reports Kossola's claim that no one died on board the *Clotilda*. Since then, some evidence has surfaced to suggest that two people did die on board and that 108 Africans made it to Alabama instead of 110, as had previously been reported.

Storytellers must make decisions. Some are seemingly simple, like word choice: We chose to use the survivors' original African names because when author Emma Langdon Roche informed the group she was writing a book about them, they requested she use their original names. Likewise, it was important to us to recognize Kossola's unique speech patterns. We chose to use "de" and "dey" to provide a sense of the dialect without overwhelming the reader. For a more complete and precise account of Kossola's dialect, please see *Barracoon: The Story of the Last "Black Cargo"* by Zora Neale Hurston.

Also, the words "slave" and "slaves" are used in this book rather than the words "enslaved people" because it's accurate to the time frame of when this story takes place.

For characters we could find little about—like second mate J. B. Northrop, for whom we only knew his name and his state of birth—we used our imaginations to create personality, motivation, and desire.

Other characters, like William Foster, we knew more about, but we also wanted to dig beyond the facts recorded in his journal. We tried to see him as a human in his time. His feelings upon hearing the slave songs while on board *Clotilda* are completely imagined. We wanted to explore that question of how people can do terrible things to other people—how could he do what he did? How did this happen? We imagined him on the edge of relating to the enslaved Africans in the hold of his ship, yet pulling away from those feelings and making a firm decision to not think of them as human—because such thoughts and his role in the story would puncture his idea of himself. Perhaps this is what some people do today when faced with people they have been taught are less than them.

As for Kossola, whose story and feelings are well-documented, it was important to us to stick to his accounts of his own story as closely as possible. Kossola loved his life and was grateful for all parts of it—in spite of the extreme violence, cruelty, and many tragedies he endured. While depicting an enslaved person experiencing gratitude may seem unlikely or impossible, Kossola's own words prove otherwise. We wanted to show this in our story to help us all recognize the incredible diversity in individuals' responses to events in life. It's important we don't create or further stereotypes of marginalized groups.

While it may seem hard to believe that Kossola and the other Africans didn't realize they were enslaved until the point in which they were part of the sale hosted by Timothy Meaher, it's true. According to Dr. Diouf, "to the Africans it was a deportation of free people followed by their enslavement" (*Dreams of Africa in Alabama*, p. 70). From the point of their capture, through their journey across the ocean, to their time in the swamps, the Africans still saw themselves as free people who had become prisoners—not enslaved.

Some characters we had to leave out entirely, for the sake of making this book a manageable read. With that in mind, we chose not to mention the birth of Kêhounco and James's first child in our narrative. Instead, we kept our focus on baby Jerry, their second child. We also chose not to include Kossola and Abilè's sons James, Pollee, or David to keep the focus on Aleck, Cudjo, Jr., and Celia. Similarly, we left out Timothy and Mary's second son (James K.) and focused only on their first son, Augustine.

Other people, like Oluale, a *Clotilda* African whose enslaved name was Charles "Charlie" Lewis, we chose to simply mention instead of adding an additional "voice." Still others, about whom little to nothing is known, or whose stories took them to other parts of the state (e.g., recently discovered *Clotilda* survivor Redoshi/Sally Smith), we were unable to fold into our narrative.

Encouraged by Dr. Diouf's findings, we made a deliberate choice to make Timothy's son Augustine more sympathetic than his father. We remain hopeful that each generation has the potential to grow and change.

We are aware that some may question whether this was our story to tell, as neither of us has direct ties to African Town. Our feeling is that it should not fall solely on the shoulders of the victims and descendants to tell any story. We need to work together and include multiple perspectives to "get it right." We connected with this story on the most human of levels and have done our best to represent as many sides as possible in our narrative. The story of Kossola and his shipmates is one of heartbreak and joy, anger and faith. We humbly hope their lives touch your spirit as much as they have ours.

Irene & Charles

VOICES

In order of appearance:

KOSSOLA [KŌ-su-la] (1841–July 17, 1935) • also known as Cudjo Lewis, nineteen years old at the time of capture from his Bantè home, which is located in the current-day country of Benin

TIMOTHY (1812–March 3, 1892) • Timothy Meaher [MAY-er], originally from Maine, owner of a shipping business located in Mobile, Alabama, who, at age forty-seven, made the bet to bring the Africans to Alabama, in spite of laws forbidding it

WILLIAM (1822–February 9, 1901) • William Foster, Canadian immigrant and shipbuilder, who was thirty-seven when hired by Timothy Meaher to captain the *Clotilda*

CLOTILDA (October 17, 1855–) • schooner built by William Foster and commissioned by Timothy Meaher to be transformed into a slave ship

J. B. (unknown birth and death years) • J. B. Northrop, second mate on board the *Clotilda*, age estimated to be mid-twenties

KÊHOUNCO [kay-YAWN-kō] (1844–April 16, 1917) • also known as Kanko or Lottie Dennison, sixteen years old when kidnapped from her home in the current-day country of Benin and brought to America aboard the *Clotilda*

GLÈLÈ [GLAY-lay] (unknown birth year–1889 or 1890) • son of Ghezo, new king of Dahomey, who captured and sold the Africans to William Foster

KUPOLLEE [KEW-pō-lee] (unknown birth year–August 19, 1922) • also known as Pollee Allen, devotee of òrìṣà, age estimated to be early twenties when captured and brought to America aboard the *Clotilda*

GUMPA (1832–September 11, 1902) • also known as Peter Lee, relative of King Glèlè, twenty-eight years old when captured and brought to America aboard the *Clotilda*

ABILÈ [ah-BEE-lay] (1845–November 14, 1908) • also known as Celia Lewis, fifteen years old when kidnapped from her home in the current-day country of Benin and brought to America aboard the *Clotilda*

JAMES (1840–October 17, 1915) • James Dennison, African American enslaved by Burns Meaher; husband of Kêhounco

MARY (1835–March 29, 1924) • Mary C. Waters Meaher, originally from Maine, the niece of one of Maine's governors (Edward Kavanaugh) and wife of Timothy Meaher

AUGUSTINE (April 24, 1861–July 29, 1938) • eldest son of Mary and Timothy Meaher

CUDJO, JR. [KEWD-jō] (1872–1902) • second-born son of Abilè and Kossola

MORE ABOUT THE CHARACTERS

What happened to the characters still living after 1901 (in alphabetical order):

ABILÈ survived the deaths of five of her six children (after the deaths of Celia and Cudjo, Jr., her sons David, Pollee, and James all died within a four-month period during 1908). She was heartbroken by the loss, and according to Kossola, she died of grief.

AUGUSTINE was the executor of his father's will and inherited the bulk of Timothy's assets, especially the real estate. (Meanwhile, son James K., living in Ohio, received $2,000). By 1905, Augustine was a multimillionaire. His death certificate and census records list his occupation as "real estate" and sometimes mention "timber." He was quite successful in expanding the family's wealth and was involved in all sorts of industrial and development projects.

The Meahers continue to be a prominent family in and around current-day Mobile, Alabama, owning a great deal of land and operating multiple businesses. Meaher Avenue runs through Africatown, and you can visit Meaher State Park, located in nearby Spanish Fort, Alabama. The family broke its decades-long silence in the February 2020 issue of *National Geographic* magazine when seventy-three-year-old Robert Meaher, the great-grandson of Timothy Meaher, said, "Slavery is wrong . . . I'll apologize." In June 2021 the Meaher family sold a former credit union building valued at $300,000 to the city for a much-reduced price of $50,000. The building will be used as offices for a new organization: Africatown Redevelopment Corporation (ARC). ARC's goals include revitalization of housing, preserving the community's history, and developing commerce in the area. Africatown residents expressed gratitude for this gesture and are hopeful that this is a first step toward opening dialogue between the Meaher family and the *Clotilda* descendants. *Source: https://www. al.com/news/2021/06/for-first-time-since-clotilda-discovery-descendants-of-slave-ships-owner-speak-out.html*

CLOTILDA was presumed destroyed by fire, so decades passed before anyone thought to search underwater for the ship. After first making a faulty claim, reporter Ben Raines discovered the actual remains of the *Clotilda* on the back side of Twelve Mile Island in April 2018. Other expeditions were conducted in cooperation with local and national organizations, including the Black Heritage Council, National Geographic Society, and the Smithsonian National Museum of African American History and Culture. The discovery was made public in May 2019.

The location of the ship proves that Timothy Meaher was untruthful in his reports (most likely in his attempt to prevent being convicted of any crimes) about where the *Clotilda* was burned. This also explains why others before Mr. Raines had been unable to find the remains of the ship. It was William Foster's journal that revealed the actual location of the *Clotilda*.

When the remains of the *Clotilda* were first (mistakenly) discovered in 2018, Hector Posset, ambassador for the Republic of Benin, visited Mobile, Alabama. Choking back sobs, he said, "I am just begging them [the shipmates] to forgive us, because we sold them. Our forefathers sold their brothers and sisters . . . May their souls rest in peace, perfect peace." *Source: https://www.al.com/news/mobile/2018/02/i_am_just_begging_them_to_forg.html*

CUDJO, JR., was shot in the throat on July 28, 1902, during a still-mysterious altercation with another man, who had been stabbed, presumably by Cudjo, Jr., himself.

GUMPA was struck by a train in an accident that seems to have been due to Mobile and Bay Shore Railroad Company's negligence and died in 1902 at age seventy. He and his wife Josephine's children included four daughters (Celia, Clara, Mary, and Polly) and three sons (Charles, James, and William).

JAMES accomplished many things, including owning a dairy farm—one of only a few black-owned businesses at the time. He and Kêhounco were still married at the time of his death (around age seventy-five).

J. B. remains a mystery. His name may have been misrecorded by William Foster. It's possible he was actually James Madison Northup, a Rhode Island–born mariner who married a woman named Penelope, had multiple children with her, and likely died at sea in 1863.

KÊHOUNCO remained self-reliant and self-employed throughout her life. In her later years, she was known for raising her famous hogs. She was preceded in death by her husband, James, sons Jerry and Willie, and daughter, Equilla. Son Napoleon assisted his mother in pursuing money due James from the Pension Bureau.

KOSSOLA rang the church bell every Sunday morning until July 26, 1935, when he died at age ninety-four of arteriosclerosis. After the deaths of Abilẹ and his children (including Aleck, who died just one month after Abilẹ in 1908), he was known to share the following parable:

"Once there was a bird beeg and strong. He have a nest of leetle birds who open they mouths, and the beeg bird feed them and they all sing happy. Then the leetle birds grow strong. The old bird get old. And open his mouth, but the birds have all fly away." *Source: "From Jungle to Slavery and Freedom: Aged Mobile Negro African Native Keeps Church" by James Saxon Childers*

During Kossola's later years he gave interviews to Emma Langdon Roche and Zora Neale Hurston, among others, which is how we know so much about his home in Bantè, how he was captured, and what happened afterward. He was long thought to be the last survivor of the *Clotilda*, until a 2019 study identified a fellow *Clotilda* survivor named Redoshi/Sally Smith who lived in Dallas County, Alabama, and died in 1937 as the last survivor. In 2020 it was announced that another shipmate, Matilda McCrear, who was just two years old at the time of the crossing, had been discovered. (In our narrative, Matilda is the two-year-old who won't stop crying in the barracoon.) Matilda died in 1940, and she is now known as the last survivor of the transatlantic slave trade.

KUPOLLEE was the father of fifteen (five with Rose, ten with Lucy). Kupollee left behind a legacy of hard work and love of land upheld by many of his descendants. He died of lobar pneumonian fever.

MARY left Alabama (and son Augustine) to live with her son James in Ohio after Timothy's death in 1892.

Other real-life characters who appear in the poems:

Abache and Sam • *Clotilda* Africans and parents of Lucy; also known as Clara and Sam Turner

Adelaide • wife of William Foster

Akodé • prince; nephew of King Glèlè

Aleck (African name: Iyadjemi) • eldest son of Abilẹ and Kossola

Andrew • enslaved person who ran away and was caught

Annie Keeby • wife of Ossa Keeby

Ausy • *Clotilda* African, also known as Ossa Keeby

Béhanzin • son of Glèlè

Burns (Meaher) • younger brother of Timothy Meaher

Bully • enslaved person

Captain Henry Romeyn • former Civil War officer

Celia (African name: Ebeossi) • daughter of Abilè and Kossola

Edward M. Robinson • lawyer

Free George • freed formerly enslaved person

Gilbert Thomas • man who died in an altercation with Cudjo, Jr.

Governor Johnson (Joseph F.) • governor of Alabama, 1896–1900

Hollingsworth (James W.) • tugboat captain

Jaba • *Clotilda* African whose enslaved name was Jaybee Jaba Shade

Jim (Meaher) • elder brother of Timothy Meaher

John Dabney • plantation owner and friend of Timothy Meaher

Jerry • son of Kêhounco and James who died at two months of age

Josephine • *Clotilda* African; wife of Gumpa

Lucy • Kupollee's second wife

Mary Woods • wife of Aleck

Mr. Ayers • businessman

Mr. Matthews • businessman

Napoleon • son of Kêhounco and James

Noah • Noah Hart, African American enslaved by Timothy Meaher

Oluale • *Clotilda* African whose enslaved name was Charles "Charlie" Lewis

Reverend Burke • minister of Stone Street Baptist Church

Reverend Phillips • visiting preacher who shared the Lord's Prayer in Yorùbá

Rose • *Clotilda* African; Kupollee's first wife

Willie • son of Kêhounco and James

William Turner • businessman

W. P. McCann • lieutenant commander of the US Navy

Fictional characters:

Adérónké • Kossola's friend and love interest in Bantè

Bridget • former enslaved person

Chaplain Fred • minister

Eniọlá • Kêhounco's older sister

Father O'Hara • priest

J. Wellington Seibert • businessman

Luke • enslaved person

Martha • former enslaved person who worked in the kitchen at Burns Meaher's house

Miss Nottingham • teacher

Mr. Deacon • businessman

Tayo • Kossola's younger half brother (he had five full siblings and twelve half siblings, but we do not know their names)

Triumphant • ship upon which J. B. Northrop was an orphaned stowaway

AFRICATOWN TODAY

Africatown (formerly known as African Town) currently consists of approximately two thousand residents in seven neighborhoods: Hog Bayou, Plateau, Magazine Point, Greens Ally, Happy Hills, Kelly Hills, and Lewis Quarters. This is down from the fourteen neighborhoods that existed up until 1970 when changes to the area, including the widening of Bay Bridge Road, the construction of the I-165 bypass, and the rezoning of property from residential to business, resulted in industrial takeover and loss of land. Factories have since closed and left behind a legacy of pollution.

The school the shipmates created eventually became the Mobile County Training School. After the school burned down in 1915, the Julius Rosenwald Foundation donated funds to rebuild. It became one of more than 5,000 schools Julius Rosenwald and Booker T. Washington built to educate freed blacks after the Civil War ended. From our research, Mobile County Training School is one of only a few Rosenwald schools still serving black children to this day.

In 1984, nine descendants of the shipmates—Eva Jones, Dell Keeby, Herman Richardson, LaDresta Green Sims, Paul Green, Melvin Wright, Lillian Autrey, Linda C. Williams Jones, and Helen Richardson Jones—formed the Clotilda Descendants Association. Its mission is to "preserve and perpetuate the culture and heritage of the last Africans brought to America . . . [and] enlighten society about their descendants and African history." *Source: theclotildastory.com*

In the 1970s the Africatown Mobilization Organization was established by friends, community members, and descendants of the *Clotilda* survivors to promote redevelopment of the area. In 2013, it was replaced by the Africatown Community and Development Corporation.

On December 4, 2012, the Africatown Historic District was named to the National Register of Historic Places.

The Africatown Heritage Preservation Foundation, founded in 2019 by Anderson Flen, Major Joe Womack, and Ruth Ballard, received a $50,000 grant from the National Trust for Historic Preservation's African American Cultural Heritage Action Fund. The funds, provided by the Andrew W. Mellon Foundation, will be used to further the group's efforts to provide "an environment of energized excellence that fosters hope, kindness, cooperation, and healing."
Source: africatownhpf.org/about-us/our-mission

In February 2020, Mobile County Commissioner Merceria Ludgood, City Councilman Levon Manzie, Mayor Sandy Stimpson, and the Alabama Historical Commission announced the latest plans to commemorate Africatown's rich history: the Africatown Heritage House, a 5,000-square-foot building on the north side of Africatown's Robert Hope Community Center and across the street from the Mobile County Training School gym. Currently under construction, the Africatown Heritage House will include a 2,500-square-foot exhibit honoring the shipmates and highlighting artifacts brought up from the *Clotilda*, as well as meeting and office space. It is scheduled to open in spring 2022.

Also in the works is a new 18,000-square-foot Africatown Welcome Center. Thanks to RESTORE Act funds, the new building will replace the current trailer across from Old Plateau Cemetery.

In May 2020, the Environmental Protection Agency selected the city of Mobile as a recipient of a $300,000 Brownfields Assessment Grant. The goal of these grants is to transform sites previously contaminated by manufacturing into community assets. Specifically, the funds from this grant will be used to assess and develop clean-up plans for the Africatown community.

In addition, the state of Alabama has committed $1 million for the preservation of the *Clotilda*.

Visitors can take a tour of Africatown arranged by the Dora Franklin Finley African American Heritage Trail. Highlights include viewing a bust of Kossola/Cudjo Lewis in front of Union Missionary Baptist Church (formerly called Old Landmark Church by the town founders), located at 506 Bay Bridge Road in Mobile, Alabama. This sculpture was created by April Livingston. At the Africatown cemetery, you can spend a moment or longer with Kossola, aka Cudjo Lewis, at a stone burial landmark. When exiting the Cochrane-Africatown USA Bridge, you can see a 15-foot impressionist mural of the *Clotilda* (spelled *Clotilde*) created by Africatown resident Labarron Lewis. Each year during the Spirit of Our Ancestors Festival, the community gathers to honor the *Clotilda* survivors and descendants. The celebration includes song, dance, and storytelling.

The descendants of the *Clotilda* survivors contribute to our society in ways rich and varied, just as their ancestors did. Social activists and advocates for justice in Africatown, they include college graduates, educators, civil servants, and more.

SELECTED TIME LINE

1808 • America bans the importation of enslaved people from Africa.

1810 • When the ban proves ineffective, the United States makes the law tougher by promising it will put violators in jail.

1835 • Timothy Meaher and Jim Meaher leave Maine and relocate in Mobile, Alabama.

October 17, 1855 • The *Clotilda* is completed and ready for its maiden voyage.

1858 • King Ghezo of Dahomey dies, and his son Badohun (called Glèlè) succeeds him.

November 9, 1858 • *Mobile Register* announces that the king of Dahomey is driving a brisk slave trade at Ouidah.

1859 • Timothy Meaher makes the bet aboard his steamer the *Roger B. Taney* as it travels up the Mobile River.

February 1860 • William Foster departs Mobile aboard the *Clotilda*.

May 1860 • William Foster arrives at Ouidah and purchases 125 kidnapped Africans between the ages of two and thirty.

July 8, 1860 • William Foster arrives in Mobile Bay with the human cargo. (Reportedly, 15 captives were left behind on the Ouidah shore, and some reports claim 2 died on the journey—in all, either 108 or 110 made it to Alabama.)

July 1860 • Timothy Meaher is arrested for the wrongful transportation of Africans to American soil. He is released when no evidence is put forth to successfully prosecute him.

April 12, 1861 • The Civil War begins.

April 24, 1861 • Augustine Meaher is born.

June 12, 1861 • Kêhounco and James are married.

October 1862 • The "Twenty Slave Law" (also called "Twenty Negro Law" and "Twenty Nigger Law") is passed. This law exempts from the draft one white man per plantation in ownership of twenty or more enslaved people.

April 9, 1865 • The Civil War ends, and the enslaved people are set free.

April 19, 1865 • James enlists in the Union Army.

November 22, 1865 • Gumpa and Kossola attend the Convention of Colored People in Mobile.

January 5, 1866 • James is released from the Union Army.

April 1866 • Kêhounco and James's baby Jerry dies.

July 4, 1867 • Aleck Lewis is born.

July 28, 1868 • The Fourteenth Amendment is ratified, granting citizenship to African Americans born in the United States.

October 1868 • The shipmates are granted US citizenship.

1870 • Residents incorporate Plateau and Magazine Point (Africa-town) with the land they purchased from the Meaher family while working for them.

1870 • Kêhounco and James purchase their own farm in Mobile.

1872 • Residents build their own church (now called Union Baptist Church).

1872 • Cudjo, Jr., is born.

Fall 1872 • More land is purchased by the shipmates to enlarge the Africatown community.

1874 • Kupollee, Kossola, and Oluale vote in Alabama state elections for the first time.

1878 • Celia Lewis is born.

1880 • Residents start a school in their church. The school eventually evolves into Mobile County Training School.

March 15, 1880 • Kossola and Abilè are married.

February 1885 • Jim Meaher dies.

1890 • Elders in the community petition the Mobile School Board to build a school.

1891 • Aleck Lewis and Mary Woods are married.

March 3, 1892 • Timothy Meaher dies.

August 5, 1893 • Celia Lewis dies.

1899 • Cudjo, Jr., is charged with manslaughter for the death of Gilbert Thomas.

January 23, 1900 • Cudjo, Jr., is convicted and sent to jail for five years.

March 13, 1900 • James and Kêhounco join the National Ex-Slave Mutual Relief, Bounty, and Pension Association.

August 7, 1900 • Cudjo, Jr., is pardoned.

1900 • Residents of the community give land to the school system to build a school (and the school system still owns the land today).

February 9, 1901 • William Foster dies.

GLOSSARY

àjànàkú • elephant

anasara • white men

àrún • five

Àwa ń lọ • We are going away

bàbá • father

bàbá àgbà • grandfather

Bantè • the town where Kossola grew up

bature • white men (Hausa language)

bẹ́ẹ̀ni • yes

ẹ̀fà • six

èje • seven

èjì • two

èjọ • eight

èrin • four

ẹ̀sán • nine

èsúsú • group savings plan in which members collect/use the total amount

ẹ̀ta • three

ẹ̀wá • ten

fùfú • starchy staple food from West Africa (Nigeria, specifically) in which crushed cassava or plantains are rolled into balls and served with soup, stewed vegetables, or other dipping sauces

gbẹ̀gìrì • a Nigerian bean soup

ilé • home

ìyá • mother

ìyá àgbà • grandmother

Kò ní séwu lọ́nà • a positive wish or prayer: "There won't be dangers on the road."

mo dúpẹ́ • thank you/I am grateful

ǹlẹ́ o • hello

ogójì • forty

ogún • twenty

òkan • one

ọkùnrin òyìnbó • white man/men

ọmọ mi • my child

òmìnira • freedom

òrìṣà • Yorùbá religion; deity

orò • group of men who collectively possess high social or political power in the Yorùbá culture

ọyé • harmattan in West Africa, the season of dust and wind (December–February)

wàrà • cheese

Yorùbá [YOH-roo-BAH] • an ethnic group that lives in Nigeria and Benin; a language; a religion; a culture

yovu • white men

POETRY FORMS/STYLES

Abilè • free-verse lines using indentation, because her words and thoughts are characterized by movement, flow, and growth.

Augustine • acrostic: The first letter of each line spells out a particular word or expression. Here, the word also acts as the poem's title. We chose this form because many children's first poems are acrostics.

Clotilda • unrhymed couplets, because on the page the stanzas look like waves.

Cudjo, Jr. • text appears in all lowercase, along with unconventional grammar (resembling the style of E. E. Cummings and Arnold Adoff); i.e., some words are smashed together, others are pulled apart. Slashes are used in place of commas. This represents his struggles in America, his efforts to create a life that blends his parents' culture and American culture, and also his willingness to break the rules.

Glèlè • extended tricube: The traditional form is defined as three stanzas that include three lines with three syllables each. Here, there are more than three stanzas. We chose this form because the poems appear stately and dignified, befitting royalty.

Gumpa • each single thought is given its own stanza, and there are few contractions. We chose this form because he is careful and proper with his words; a leader who takes great care with language.

James • no-pivot tanka. Five-line stanzas with a syllable count per line: 5-7-5-7-7. There's no pivot line on the third line like in a usual tanka. We chose this ancient, elegant form and gave it a twist, because in many ways James is an old soul with progressive ideas (like about gender roles—he encourages Kêhounco's independence and considers her an equal, even when it was not common at the time to do so).

J. B. Northrop • three-line, free-verse stanzas, since he's third in command on the ship.

Kêhounco • cherita, a narrative poem with three stanzas. The first one-line stanza sets the scene, and it's followed by a two-line stanza, then a third. We chose this form because she was a "watcher" more than a talker—when she does talk, every word matters.

Kossola • long, free-verse, left-aligned poems, because Kossola was a storyteller.

Kupollee • nonet, a nine-line poem with nine syllables on the first line, then eight on the second line, going down by syllable count in descending order. Or the reverse. Rhyming optional. Sometimes, when Kupollee had more to say, a double-nonet. We chose this form because he's a gardener, and each nonet poem starts or ends with a seed (one-syllable word) and blooms (or withers).

Mary • triolet, an eight-line poem where the first, fourth, and seventh lines repeat themselves and the second line repeats itself in the final line, because she is a society woman, and the repetition in this form resembles music and dance.

Timothy • centered free verse, because he was verbose and enjoyed being the center of the attention.

William • free-verse, right-aligned, five-line stanzas, to visually resemble a ship's log.

LEARN MORE ABOUT THE SHIPMATES, THE *CLOTILDA*, AND AFRICAN TOWN

Books

Ajapa and the Tortoise: A Book of Nigerian Folk Tales by Margaret Baumann (Dover Publications, 2003)

Barracoon: The Story of the Last "Black Cargo" by Zora Neale Hurston (Amistad, 2018)

Dreams of Africa in Alabama: The Slave Ship Clotilda *and the Story of the Last Africans Brought to America* by Sylviane A. Diouf (Oxford University Press, 2007)

Historic Sketches of the South by Emma Langdon Roche (The Knickerbocker Press, 1914; available online: archive.org/details/historicsketches01roch/page/n7/mode/2up)

The Last Slave Ship by Ben Raines (Simon & Schuster, 2022)

The Slave Ship Clotilda *and the Making of Africatown, USA: Spirit of Our Ancestors* by Natalie S. Robertson (Praeger, 2008)

Magazines

"Last Journey into Slavery," cover article in February 2020 issue of *National Geographic*; available online: nationalgeographic.com/magazine/article/clotilda-americas-last-slave-ship-stole-them-from-home-it-couldnt-steal-their-identities-feature

Online

Africatown listed as a UNESCO Site of Memory: middlepassageproject.org

C.H.E.S.S. blog (about current happenings in Africatown): africatown-chess.org

Clotilda Descendants Association:
theclotildastory.com

Learn about Matilda McCrear (last survivor of the transatlantic slave trade):
bbc.com/news/education-52010859; nationalgeographic.com/history/2020/03/last-slave-ship-survivor-descendants-identified

Learn Yorùbá:
youtube.com/Yorubalessons

Local coverage about the discovery of the remains of *Clotilda*:
lagniappemobile.com/sunken-treasure-a-reporters-remarkable-account-of-finding-the-last-slave-ship/

On the Media podcast on African Town:
wnycstudios.org/podcasts/otm/episodes/africatown [54 minutes long; starts at 4 minutes, 30 seconds]

Smithsonian Magazine coverage about the discovery of the remains of *Clotilda*:
smithsonianmag.com/smithsonian-institution/clotilda-last-known-slave-ship-arrive-us-found-180972177

The Architectural League's American Roundtable "If We Can Save the Ship, We Can Save the Town" project:
archleague.org/article/africatown-intro

Videos

Deborah Plant, editor of Zora Neale Hurston's *Barracoon: The Story of the Last "Black Cargo,"* discusses the book:
c-span.org/video/?473005-1/barracoon-story-black-cargo

Dr. Henry Louis Gates's *Finding Your Roots*, about drummer Ahmir "Questlove" Thompson's connection to Africatown:
time.com/5057004/questlove-finding-roots-last-slave-ship

National Geographic Channel *Drain the Oceans* episode "Drain America's Last Slave Ship":
imdb.com/title/tt10925886/?ref_=ttep_ep1

60 Minutes "Africatown" segment, November 29, 2020:
cbsnews.com/amp/news/clotilda-slave-ship-alabama-60-minutes-2020-11-29/

Joe Womack talks about the history of Africatown:
youtu.be/3Y69lYVXkeo

What the discovery of the last American slave ships means to descendants:
nmaahc.si.edu/explore/initiatives/africatown-alabama-usa

"*Clotilda*'s on Fire," a song by Shemekia Copeland, from album titled *Uncivil War*, featuring award-winning musician and Alabama native Jason Isbell:
youtu.be/nJh-eq3WGuc

ACKNOWLEDGMENTS

We are grateful to so many who helped us on our *African Town* journey. First and foremost to our editor extraordinaire, Stacey Barney, for believing in this story even when it was just an unfinished idea.

Further gratitude to the team at G. P. Putnam's Sons: Rebecca Aidlin, Richard Amari, Danielle Ceccolini, Elaine Christina Damasco, Diane João, Cindy Howle, Deborah Kaplan, Catherine Karp, Caitlin Tutterow, and Olivia Russo. Thanks also to Vivian Shih for her thoughtful illustrations.

This wouldn't be a book without the scholars and passionate people whose work made way for ours, most especially Robert Battles, Sylviane A. Diouf, Zora Neale Hurston, Ben Raines, Natalie S. Robertson, Emma Langdon Roche, Henry C. Williams, Joe Womack, and Lorna Gail Woods.

Thanks to those who welcomed and educated us about Africatown while we were in Mobile, including Eric Finley of the Dora Franklin Finley African-American Heritage Trail; the History Museum of Mobile; Nancy Milford; and everyone at Kazoola Eatery & Entertainment.

Special thanks to Adérónkẹ Babajide for fact-checking us on all things Yorùbá. Any remaining mistakes are ours alone.

Much gratitude to Kathy Erskine for reading an early draft and providing invaluable feedback.

Deep appreciation to Joycelyn M. Davis for her kindness in writing the introduction to this book, and for her tireless work in helping make sure the lives of the *Clotilda* Africans will never be forgotten.

Major shout-outs to Ann Biggs and Valerie Ellis at the Mobile Library of Local History and Genealogy for answering our litany of questions with such generosity and specificity.

Additional thanks to the following people and institutions for their guidance and good cheer: Lynn Baker, Skip Busby, Tammy Busby, Foley Art Center, Jillian Girardeau, Felice Michael Harris, Mary Hughs, Andrew Latham, Daniel Latham, Eric Latham, Paul Latham, Heather Leonardi, Mia Manekofsky, Christian Noble, Denny Price, Zana Price, Schomburg Center for Research in Black Culture, Camija Salic, Jamie Simpkins, Traci Sorell, Rosemary Stimola, Lauren Tennyson, Paula Bantom Waters, and Chandra Wright.

Finally, thank you to our readers for joining us on this journey.

Eric Latham

Irene Latham & Charles Waters are "Poetic Forever Friends" first and collaborators second. They are the writing team behind *Can I Touch Your Hair? Poems of Race, Mistakes, and Friendship*, which was awarded a Charlotte Huck Honor, and *Dictionary for a Better World: Poems, Quotes, and Anecdotes from A to Z*, an NCTE Notable Poetry Book. They share a passion for poetry and are committed to creating meaningful books for young readers. This is their first novel together.

Visit them online at

irenelatham.com

charleswaterspoetry.com